I Sweep
the Sun
off Rooftops

Also by Hanan al-Shaykh

The Story of Zahra

Women of Sand and Myrrh

Beirut Blues

Only in London

I Sweep the Sun off Rooftops

Stories by

Hanan al-Shaykh

Translated by Catherine Cobham

BLOOMSBURY

First published in the United States by Doubleday,
a division of the Bantam Doubleday Dell Publishing Group, Inc., 1986

This paperback edition published by Bloomsbury Publishing Plc 2002

'I Sweep the Sun off Rooftops', 'The Funfair',
'The Keeper of the Virgins' and 'The Scratching of Angels' Pens'
were previously published by Allen & Unwin in 1994.

Bloomsbury Publishing Plc, 38 Soho Square, London W1D 3HB

A CIP catalogue record is available from the British Library

ISBN 0 7475 6131 1

10 9 8 7 6 5 4 3 2 1

Printed in Great Britain by Clays Ltd, St Ives plc

Contents

I Sweep
the Sun
off Rooftops

A Season of Madness

I fell upon my mother-in-law, biting her nose. I had always hated her nose. The day before I had banged the door in her face and emptied the rubbish bin on her from the balcony as she went to get in the car and drive away. I scattered frangipani blossoms over her and sang to her and put a garland of jasmine around her neck, pulling her toward me and kissing her face and hands and her silk scarf. I took the scarf off her and spread it out on the floor and asked her why we did not hire one of the horse-drawn carriages printed on it. Some of the time she tried to escape from me and other times she composed herself and made some effort to bring me to my senses, then despaired and looked up at the ceiling, pleading with God to tell her what she had done to deserve a mad daughter-in-law. "I only chose her as a wife for my son because she came from one of the best families," she protested.

My response was to kick my legs high in the air, demanding to know why I felt so hot, and praying for ice cubes to cool me down, holding out my skirt to receive them. My husband rushed over and tried to pull my skirt over my bare legs and I struggled and bit his hand. All he said as he steered me toward my room was "Is this really how you want us to live, Fatin?"

The two of them finally pushed me into my room and I sat staring at my reflection in the mirror and laughed at my appearance in disbelief. I heard them commiserating with each other over the state of the house, his bad luck in marrying me, and the children's distress at seeing their mother losing her mind.

His mother suggested taking me to a doctor locally, while he favored sending me back to Lebanon. They debated whether this would provoke too much of a scandal, then he pronounced that I would be a source of shame whichever they did, for I already was, even within those four walls: I wore no protection during my periods; I calculated how many eyelashes I had, using a pencil to separate them; I stuck flowers in the front of my shoes; I threw things away regardless of their value; I had tried to jump out of the window and fly, and run away in a truck transporting ivory, clinging on to the tusks until the driver found me and handed me over to the police.

I stumbled along in my madness, never meeting my real self except when my eyes fell on the watercolors, which the strange light in this African country had inspired me to paint; it was a light that broke the hold of the sun's burning rays for a short time at daybreak and dusk. I often wondered if I should tear these paintings down from the walls, in case they were what made my husband keep hoping that the old Fatin would return. (She was the girl who could not even say yes when she was asked to be his bride because, as well as being shy, she was dazzled by the fact that the offer was coming from a member of a wealthy emigrant family.) What really happened was that I did not think too much about whether to accept or refuse. If I finally said yes, it was probably because I was distracted by his mother's gold bracelet, wondering what logic could possibly lie behind the choice of the charms dangling from it: an acorn, a house, a heart, a mountain, the Lebanese flag and a tortoise.

All I could hear now was my mother-in-law—she who

was used to finding an answer to everything—questioning, scolding, complaining because he could not decide what to do about me, while he merely repeated, "God help us," in resigned tones.

I felt more hopeful when the doctor came. He asked them to describe how my condition had worsened and if some incident had sparked it. "The sea," answered my mother-in-law. "It began that time she went to the sea and it poured with rain."

Then he turned to me and asked me my age. "The age of madness," I replied.

This answer ensured that he never addressed me again. He asked them if there was any mental illness in my family. When they both shook their heads, I interrupted and said they were lying: they knew about my aunt; the cause of her madness remained a mystery and she had been moved from one psychiatric unit to another. I described how my mother had made me take her a dish of tabbouleh one day, and how she had pushed me against the wall and forced me to swap clothes with her, threatening to kill me if I opened my mouth. She had gone home in my place, slept in my bed, gone to school, played with my friends, married a man living in Africa and had hundreds of children with him. Although she visited Lebanon often, she had never come to visit me in the clinic. I fell silent briefly when I noticed the doctor leaving the room, then renewed my efforts, and screamed and howled and meowed and brayed and struck my face and banged on the window.

The saga continued and I could no longer bear the passing of time. I was worn out by the waiting and the madness. I decided that in order to resolve the situation I would have to develop my madness and become dangerous.

"She's crazy. The doctor's confirmed it," shouted my mother-in-law. "I guessed as much. Even when she was sane, her eyes had signs of it. I'll find you another wife once we've sent her back to her family. Let them pay for her to be treated. The children will be all right at their boarding schools." Then she lowered her voice and said very quietly, "Marriage is like everything else in life—a matter of luck. Who says a worm-eaten apple can't look red and juicy from the outside?"

I listened intently as I floated above the wooden floor, and sank, and tried to rise again. His voice drowned out hers, accusing her of being hard and selfish. He swore he would never marry again, because he was not going to leave me: he could not forget how I used to be when I was well. Marriage was for better or worse. He would have me cured. He loved me, he would never make me look ridiculous by sending me back to my family. He would stand by me. I shook my head, rejecting his compassion, floating farther away. His mother was temporarily infected by my madness and screamed maniacally at him: "I'm telling you she'll kill you. She'll poison you. She'll tear you apart with her teeth. Can't you see she's turned into a crazy bitch? She'll burn you alive, or stick a knife in you while you're asleep."

Encouraged by her reaction, I became more absorbed in my madness, rising and falling, then floating again, borne along by the sweat that was pouring off me. I heard him shouting back at her, pushing her away, and vowing not to abandon me even if I did take a knife to him. She exploded with rage, trying to make him see that he must extricate himself from my power, for I had procured charms from the magicians at the seaside, where I used to go sketching, and had planned out his fate for him.

"I'll never leave her. Never," he interrupted. "I'd give up the world for her."

When I heard this, I directed my energies to calming myself down, and took the last escape route left open to me: I washed my face, tied back my hair, fastened my robe modestly around me as I used to in the past, and went out to them in the filigree sandals that I had not worn since I went mad. I sat facing them, utterly composed, disregarding their eyes, which stood out from their faces with lives of their own, but full of panic. My calmness made them flex their arms and legs, ready to ward off any sudden attacks, or run for their lives.

But I hesitated, not knowing where to start. Should I tell them that I had been content like any wife, firmly convinced that life was marriage, children, running a house, sex from time to time, and secretly retiring inside myself when I wanted to question my feelings, or a certain melody made me happy or sad? I had begun to snatch some time to draw and paint, and eventually another man had come into my life. He used to watch me regularly as I sat facing the sea, trying to transfer the color of it onto the paper in front of me, and would pick up everything I left behind me, even raking up the colored chalk dust with his fingernails, seeing this scavenging as hugely important. I could feel that my life had changed, and everything around me began to have some meaning: the temperature of the seawater lapping around my feet; his liking for the misshapen nail on my little toe; the glass of fruit juice in his hand; silence interspersed with talk, sleep with anxiety. The time came when he could pass his hand over my face without touching it, and I would feel a great warmth suffusing me and my heart beating faster, and when I stopped being able to force myself to leave these sensations behind as I reluctantly entered the other world which was in full swing at home. Although all aspects of this world—from the salt cellar and pepper pot to the place of my burial when my time was up—ran through everything I did, everything except breathing freely from the heart, I decided to loose the threads from the cocoon of marriage one by one, taking great care to ensure that none snapped or changed color. What I really wanted was for my husband to discover that he had no choice but to leave me.

I began by handing him the soap, pretending to forget that this is said to be a sign of an imminent parting. I kissed his eyes while he slept, disregarding the song that says, "Don't kiss me on my eyes, or tomorrow we'll be separated"; I took care that the toes of his shoes were always pointing toward the front door. Nevertheless, my husband continued to live his life as normal both at home and at work, so I had no choice but to make him revolted by me. Without much effort I turned myself into a human dustbin: I drank milk as if it were water, although I was allergic to it. I encouraged my guts to swell up with it, and with the cabbage, cauliflower and pulses that I also ate in large quantities. I swallowed garlic cloves as if they were pieces of chocolate, crunched onions as if they were sweet-smelling carrots, and then went to bed without brushing my teeth. While I was waiting for my husband to join me, I belched incessantly, releasing the pent-up gases whose odor spread through the surrounding air.

However, I always found my husband at my side when I woke up in the morning. He stayed, despite my acts of rebellion and constant questioning of my life with him. Why did nature not do its job and make him disappear, or rescue me from the pit I was in and cast me out into the world?

When nothing changed, and after periods of thought that were agitated, calm, logical and reckless by turns, I decided upon madness.

But I did not disclose all this to them now; I found myself confessing to them in a low voice, articulating very clearly, that I was not mad, but afraid and ashamed because I had fallen in love with another man and wanted a divorce so that I could marry him. I asked them to forgive me for pretending to be mad because my husband's good-heartedness and generous nature had stopped me from telling the truth, which was that I had never loved him all the time I lived with him and had feared that the knowledge of this might fester inside him, a wound refusing to heal. My conscience had eaten away at me on account of my unfaithfulness to him, and I had believed that my contrived madness would prompt him to remove me from his life without any qualms—indeed, he would welcome the prospect. I added that I was determined to ask for a divorce but wanted nothing from them, not even the Beirut apartment, which was in my name. As I said this, I realized that my mother-in-law was the one I feared most. Then I forced myself to look up and confront them. All the time I was giving an honest account of myself I had been staring at the floor. Now I fixed my eyes on their faces to prove to them how strong and brave I was, whatever their reactions might be. I waited for one of them to respond, expecting reproaches, physical blows, retribution of some kind, convincing myself that I would escape from them, regardless of the outcome.

Then his mother was clasping my hand, twisting her mouth into a grimace of pity and murmuring, "She's crazy, poor thing. Nothing can be done for her."

My husband collapsed, burying his face in his hands and repeating sadly, "Poor thing, she's so young. I swear to God, I'll take her anywhere in the world to find a cure for her."

The Spirit Is Engaged Now (Do You Want to Hold?)

Even though the occasion was so important to me, I tried to avoid it. I woke up in the night, boiling hot, certain that I had a temperature. I wanted desperately to be ill enough to have to stay in bed, to shiver and have aching joints and a headache so bad that I could think of nothing else but how to relieve the pain. But my daughter's call from the States meant I didn't have the opportunity to play the sick ostrich. My conversation with her forced me out of bed, and I dragged myself across the room and pulled a dress out from the bottom of the wardrobe, where winter and summer clothes lay jumbled together with shoes, handbags and jewelry.

I chose a dress my husband used to like on me, and thought how my daughter's absence had made it easier for me to live in this mess. I blessed it as I saw the empty hangers and thought of the creeping chaos in various parts of the house.

I wanted to be able to wake up happy after good dreams or panic-stricken after nightmares with no one watching me and telling me to cheer up all the time. It was too easy for people to dismiss the angry or the vulnerable with phrases like "Take it easy" or "You'll have forgotten about it before long," I thought, as I pulled the dress on. It was many months since I had worn it and I felt throttled by it; I tore it off as if I were detaching a leech from my skin, dropped it on the floor and burst into tears. Then I picked it up and put it back on, forcing myself to be calm: I was trying to keep my thoughts under control but I couldn't help imagining my husband looking out on the gathering from a house or a car. The idea made me desperate, but unexpectedly my thoughts took a more positive turn, and I felt the urge to take some trouble over my appearance so that I wouldn't have to listen to my family saying, "What have you been doing to yourself?" or "If only she'd do something about herself. It's hard to believe we raised her."

Today the street where my mother used to live was going to be named after her. She had been one of the leading figures on the stage, famous for her acting and her extraordinary personality, even though she had been married and divorced four times and her fifth husband was roughly my age. Her talent and the fact that she was serious about her work had saved her from attacks on her private life. I had been told that a representative of the government would be there and someone from the ministry of arts. I wondered how they were going to fix the nameplate on the wall. Life was unfair. They appreciated creative artists either when they had one foot in the grave or after they were dead. My mother had not taken it in when she had been given an award for her acting, even though she had still been alive as far as those around her were concerned. In her own mind, she had as good as died when she learned she had an incurable illness. I remember holding her hand and thinking it felt like a bunch of bones. She had begged me not to let anyone come into the room.

Everything about her had changed, even her facial features, to the extent that she no longer recognized herself in the mirror. When I put the award down beside her, I thought she was snoring or giggling until she murmured, "I'd gladly exchange it for one hour without pain." Then I realized she had been crying.

I stood in the street, enjoying the company of theatrical

friends of my mother whom I had known since childhood, and was glad that I hadn't managed to be ill, until various members of my family started to appear. Among them were my mother's brothers, who had broken off relations with her for many years following her decision to go on the stage, and then made it up with her when she became famous. There they were, sipping their fruit juice proudly and reveling in their status. They tried to approach me and I avoided their eyes, afraid that they would invite me back to their homes after the ceremony.

I had no desire to hear them telling me how uneasy they were at the kind of life I was living. I was among friends, people my mother had been on stage with and all her ex-husbands; the traffic in the surrounding streets and curious children, who wanted to drink the juice but had no idea what was going on, provided a protective blanket of sound. But I felt the sting of their sidelong glances, and my conversation faltered as I wondered whether to pretend to look overwhelmed by the event or cheerful and relaxed, and wavered uneasily between the two. Although the idea horrified me, I couldn't help scanning the mostly familiar faces, then raising my eyes to the windows and balconies searching for my husband. He was out of my mind only briefly when the audience burst into enthusiastic applause.

The government representative fixed the sign to the wall. "Amina Salim Street," it said. A woman standing beside Tante Samia let out a trill of joy and tears came into my eyes. Tante Samia herself clapped her hands as vigorously as a young woman. The government deputy climbed down off the chair he had been standing on with some difficulty, almost losing his balance, and Tante Samia rushed to take advantage of his discomfiture, seizing his hand and then whipping off her spectacles to show him her eyes. I heard snatches of what she was saying to him: ". . . cataract . . . operation . . . times are difficult . . . the country ought to remember its old artists."

They were certainly old. All those who were able to travel had attended the ceremony. Public transportation was bad enough for the healthy, so what must it be like for the old and sick and poor? They were happy to be there, although some of them were unable to express it because they were ill or wretched or caught up in remembering the past and their youth. They looked like a troupe of wandering players without a stage or an audience or even the price of a ticket to go from one place to the next. They weren't the same as the rest of the guests: their faces looked different and they wore strange clothes that, although they were old and shabby, still had an air of nobility and a touch of the fantastic about them. Perhaps they were clothes they had worn on stage, Amm Badir's in particular: he wore a baggy white suit, spotted with rust, and a straw hat without a brim.

When darkness had fallen and the guests were leaving, Tante Samia put her arm around me and said, "Come on! Let's go to your place. We must tell Amina what's been happening. It'll cheer her up a bit."

I turned to look at her in alarm. Had she too begun to mix up people and events? Recently I had grown used to hearing the strangest and most wretched talk from friends of my mother's whom I met by chance. They would take my hand and ask me if Amina was getting better, even though they had been at her funeral, or when I introduced myself to them they wouldn't know who my mother was. Tante Samia refused to let go of me, and in the end I found myself welcoming her persistence because members of my family were pressing me to be with them that evening and I was able to assure them that I had to stay with her. They looked at me reproachfully, unable to believe that I preferred her company to theirs, and she must have seemed a pathetic creature to them: she wore a fox fur draped around her shoulders, whose face and ears were eaten away, and whose hairs were molting all over her clothes. One had come to rest on her lower lip, and most of her front teeth were missing. Then their accusing eyes shifted to Tante Samia's friend, Nazik, who was having difficulty staying upright, much less walking, in her platform shoes.

I didn't know how to reply to Tante Samia when she kept saying how happy she was that she would be able to take the news to Amina. To change the subject I lied and told her I was thinking of writing a biography of my mother. What did she think of the idea?

"You're a dutiful daughter. I'll do what I can to help. I've got lots of memories, cuttings, photos."

I felt ashamed of myself for doubting her sanity, or thinking she might be mixing my mother up with my daughter, who was also called Amina.

"We can tell her you're going to write a book about her too," she added.

Again I decided she must have lost her mind, and felt suddenly annoyed and tired. I wished I could escape from them without causing offense, and began complaining of my aches and pains.

"We'll give you a massage," she exclaimed tenderly, "and make you some mutton broth to help you sleep."

I felt sorry for them, but I was secretly amused at the thought of their old hands massaging me. As we walked along I told her that I felt much better, and that it must have been all the standing about. I remembered what a mess I had left the flat in as I unlocked the door, but reassured myself with the thought that Samia's mind was confused and her sight poor, and I didn't know Nazik.

"Please have a seat." I indicated the sofa, picking my nightdress off it. "Make yourselves comfortable."

But they didn't respond.

They both stood looking around the sitting room, then Tante Samia hurried over to the dining table and felt its surface. "Don't worry, my dear. The table's better!"

Then she seized hold of the tablecloth and said, "Look! Amina's tablecloth! What a loyal daughter you are!"

I excused myself for a moment and went into my room. What if I lay on the bed and went to sleep or read a book? I knew I was deluding myself, but I wanted to be alone and soak up all the memories of the day, which had been a culmination of such a large slice of the past.

I heard Tante Samia asking Nazik to draw the curtains. She could no longer distinguish between night and day. I regretted letting them come with me, but then wavered again as I remembered all Tante Samia had done for my mother. Bracing myself, I got up. "What would you like to drink?" I asked them.

Tante Samia lit a cigarette. "Don't go to any trouble, dear," she said. "Something cold. Lemonade will do fine."

When she noticed that I was still waiting for an answer from Nazik, who was searching busily through her bag, she gave a dismissive wave of her hand. "Don't worry. Nazik will have the same as me."

They both downed their lemonade in one gulp and Nazik immediately rose to her feet and picked up the glasses. I begged her not to bother, but she insisted. "The table must be empty. Who knows, something might get broken."

Tante Samia leaned close and spoke in a low voice. "You should wash your hands. We must be pure in the spirit's presence. Forgive me for asking, but you don't have a period or anything like that, do you?"

From her bag Nazik produced a square wooden board and a fine china coffee cup without a handle. The letters of the alphabet and the words *yes* and *no* were inscribed on the board, and in the middle of it was a circle; I had seen classmates of mine with exactly the same thing, made out of paper.

"Wood? Not paper?" I heard myself say.

"Paper?" repeated Tante Samia. "Do you think people have time to make a new one each day?"

I decided I would leave them to it and fetch my book. My attitude toward calling up spirits hadn't changed. At school I had marveled at its popularity, as I was busy with the living people around me. The dead were an illusion. In those years none of my relations had died, nobody I loved, not even anyone I knew. I remembered my incredulity when a boy who had been chasing me for months finally had an excuse to talk to me, and chose instead to join the others calling up the spirits and talking to the dead. But those days when I was bursting with life had passed. Now that I was moribund, I had no desire to spend time with others like me, and being a spectator at such activities required too much effort.

However, Tante Samia and Nazik considered my presence as an indication that I was happy to participate, and Tante Samia told me to place my index finger on the rim of the cup. She recited some verses from the Quran while Nazik put her finger on the other side of the cup, which appeared to be imprisoned inside the circle on the board. Then Samia summoned my mother's spirit.

"If you're there, say yes," she called.

The cup moved, making a slight whispering sound, and my finger moved with it. It came to rest on the word *yes*. Tante Samia's features relaxed and she cried, "I've really missed you, Amina."

"You shouldn't say you've missed her," whispered Nazik. "It's bad luck."

"Hallo, Amina. It's been a long time," continued Samia. "Today we had a celebration for you. They named the place where you used to live after you. The whole of Cairo was jumping. All the ministers and their deputies were there, and there were flags in the street, and music."

She winked at me, as if to apologize for her exaggerations, or rather her lies, and then went on, "Can you hear me?" The cup moved again to the word *yes*.

"Congratulations! Many congratulations!"

Then Tante Samia went on talking as if she were on the telephone. Her red lipstick looked ridiculous. I pictured my mother getting fed up with her: her spirit would be yawning by now. Tante Samia went on without any change in her tone, "We're in your daughter's house. Yes, she's here with us, she'll say hallo. But, tell me, are you pleased about the news?"

The cup moved to *yes,* and then to the letters *V-E-R-Y.*

"What did she say?" Tante Samia asked us, trying to follow the cup. When her face was almost touching the board, Nazik pushed it away and shouted, "She says she's very pleased."

Tante Samia then put her finger on the cup to take my place. "Your turn now, dear," she said.

I forced a few tears out and shook my head.

"Your daughter seems upset," she resumed. "Never mind. You can go away now, Amina."

She recited a few more verses from the Quran, then the timbre of her voice changed as she said, almost crossly, "Come on, Nazik, it's your turn, and then mine again."

Nazik looked unenthusiastic, but called upon her mother's spirit a couple of times before saying in a hopeless voice, "I knew there wouldn't be an answer. Perhaps her spirit's lost or something."

It was true, the cup was motionless on the board. She tried again. She exhaled noisily, then said, "What if I summon that man who appeared to us once before? What was his name? Fadil."

"What man? Who's Fadil?" demanded Tante Samia impatiently.

"The man who answered us by mistake when I was summoning my mother's spirit. The last time we tried it."

"Oh, I remember," said Tante Samia in a bored voice.

Nazik called on him again to ask about her mother. "I'm her daughter. I spoke to you last time. Please, let me talk to her. I'm waiting."

Then the cup moved and she bent over it, reading the letters it spelled out. *"E-N-G-A-G-E-D.* What did you say? *Engaged?* That's impossible. Oh, she's not there?"

Tante Samia removed her cigarette agitatedly from between her lips. "He's making fun of us. Talking to someone else! Not in! Where's she going to go? That's the first time I've heard of a spirit being busy. It's impossible. She must still be annoyed with you, Nazik. Don't take no for an answer. Tell him she must be angry because you buried her in Cairo instead of her hometown. Let him explain to her that it was so that you could visit her more often."

Nazik repeated Tante Samia's words parrot-fashion to the spirit Fadil, and the two of them waited for the cup to move. When nothing happened, Nazik dismissed the man's spirit and sat looking vague.

Had my finger really moved over the letters, endowed

with the spirit's ferocious energy, or was it Nazik or Tante Samia dragging the cup along? Although I swung between credulity and disbelief, images of figures in white sheets continued to float through my mind.

I was brought back to reality by the sound of Tante Samia calling on the spirit of her nephew Afeef. Her voice was different this time, tearful and imploring. She asked him how he was, if there was anyone with him, and whether he could hear her clearly. When the cup stopped on the word *yes,* she wept, asking him to forgive her, then regained her composure and dried her face on her sleeve. How small her pupils looked, like pinheads! She put her glasses back on so that she could talk seriously and give him detailed news of his children, Ahmad, Muhammad, Mustafa and Nora, tell him what marks they'd got in school, and report that their mother, his wife, was as mean as ever, God forgive her.

She apologized for saying this, then rattled on. "We slaughtered a sheep at the Feast. We fed it on early clover to fatten it up. I'm talking to you from Amina's daughter's place. Amina had a street named after her. The minister was there and he said he'd seen me on stage and was an admirer of mine. I talked to him because of the cataract operation."

I felt the cup being pulled along with unaccustomed force. Even Nazik felt it and shouted, "Come on, Samia, let him go. He's fed up. He's pulling the cup."

Tante Samia paused for breath, then asked quickly, "Are you in a hurry, dear? Good-bye. Take care of yourself, dear."

Then she dismissed him and turned to us, yelling hysterically, her painted mouth and dark glasses strangely at odds with her grief. "I know he hasn't forgiven me. Did you see how much of a hurry he was in? He hasn't forgiven me. He's right. Before he died he said to me, 'I'm ill, Auntie.' I didn't believe him. No one did. He started to walk with a stick and he couldn't stop shaking. I imitated him, and everybody laughed. A week before he died, he said to me, 'Let me stay with you for a few days, Auntie, with my family, until things sort themselves out.' I wouldn't have him. I said a few days will turn into a few years and told him to look for a job. He had a bad reputation. Horses and the lottery. He's right not to forgive me. The poor man gambled to get money to live on."

"Heavens! It's nine o'clock!" said Nazik, looking at her watch. She picked up the board and returned it to her bag. I felt anxious. I had become involved with what was going on in the room and almost ceased to be a spectator. I no longer wondered whether Nazik was cheating and pulling the cup toward the letters that suited her. I was trying to work out the reasons for my change of heart, to understand what Samia and Nazik were doing. They wanted to arrive at some point of reconciliation with the dead, so that they could be at peace with the living.

My head was starting to hurt. Hesitantly I asked Tante Samia if I would be able to summon the spirit of someone precious to me without speaking out loud.

"Why not, dear?" answered Tante Samia briskly. "Nazik and I will go out on the balcony." Then, checking herself, she went on, "No, you can't do it alone. What if you talk to the spirit in your head? I'm sure it would be able to hear you."

"She can't. That's not allowed," interrupted Nazik.

Tante Samia turned to her sharply. "Of course she can't," she said sarcastically. "Otherwise you won't be able to hear what's said and that'll keep you awake all night. You're so nosy!"

Nazik shrugged her shoulders indifferently. "Do as you please," she said.

I felt hot with embarrassment at what I was thinking of saying, then I seemed to hear a voice ordering me to speak.

"Is it true that you were sorry you left me?" I whispered.

The cup shot across the board. When I saw it landing on the word *yes,* I relaxed.

My voice grew louder. "Was Sana the one who . . . ?"

Yes.

"Did you know you had a bad heart before you divorced me?"

No.

"Did you divorce me because you'd stopped loving me altogether?"

No.

"Do you love her?"

No.

"Do you love me?"

Yes.

My eyes flew from one side of the board to the other as if I were watching a tennis ball, and the sweat ran down my back.

"Are you sorry?"

Yes. Yes.

I burst into tears and tried to leave the table, but Tante Samia protested, at first in a stifled, fearful voice, then with a shriek that made me drop back into my seat.

"You mustn't leave the spirit suspended in the cup, child. Say good-bye to it. Dismiss it."

I sobbed uncontrollably.

"God help us," she shouted, struggling to compose herself. "The spirit's still hanging in the cup, child."

She said a prayer, recited a few verses from the Quran, said another prayer. "The spirit doesn't want to go. You'll have to dismiss it yourself." Then she started to shout:

"Please, I know what I'm talking about. Once the spirit of a woman we didn't know turned up by mistake and stayed with us the whole night."

The two women began repeating "In the Name of God the Compassionate, the Merciful" in chorus. The fear that dominated their faces frightened me, but I buried my head in my hands, hoping they'd go away and leave me. I was thinking, If his spirit stays around, I can talk to it instead of listening to the radio all the time.

Since he left me, the radio had become my constant companion. Samia and Nazik were trying to pull my hands away from my face. I could smell Samia's breath and feel her spit spraying over me. They shook me, gently at first, then more violently. I didn't respond to them. Better to have his spirit to talk to than to debate constantly with myself about him, being too easy on myself sometimes and on him at others, exaggerating either the love or the unkindness.

Samia slapped my face. "That's to bring you to your senses. Do you feel better now? The spirit's still hanging in the cup. You must dismiss it. Please."

He had told our daughter to give me a tranquilizer and force me to come to the hospital so that he could say good-bye. I hadn't believed her. So he had died loving me. Sana herself had admitted as much to my daughter.

I heard Tante Samia reciting verses from the Quran and ordering the spirit to leave. I had the impression she was doing it over and over again. "It won't go," she shouted, almost sobbing by now.

Then Nazik intervened. She seemed to think she could outsmart the spirit and said loudly, "Go easy on him, Samia! Don't you know it's her husband she's talking to? How can he leave her? Her face is as beautiful as the moon. I'm sure he's not going to go unless she tells him to. Don't forget that she was the one who summoned him."

If he didn't want to leave me now, how had he managed to tell me that he couldn't live without Sana, my best friend, and make me feel as if I had been wrung out like laundry? I hadn't said good-bye to him or gone to his funeral. I hadn't grieved and wept with the others and so his death had remained an unsolved riddle, an event on the borders of reality.

Samia slapped me again. A rock that had been sitting on my chest for months had suddenly rolled off. Another slap, and Tante Samia was shouting, "Dismiss the spirit, girl. For my sake, and Nazik's. We've got other relatives we want to stay in contact with. Do you want me to get a bad reputation in the spirit world?"

If only they would leave me at this table, where we used to eat. I can see his hands resting on it now, nursing his glass of whisky, his newspaper spread out in front of him. He used to sit on that chair, although he was always ready to offer it to visitors, because it was the most comfortable. He would put old records of Umm Kulthum on the turntable, and her voice would echo sweetly around the room. If only these two weeping, wailing women, afraid for the spirit suspended in the cup, would leave me now. I want it to stay there. I've lived through years of love and marriage with it.

I used to be possessed with a desire to be near him even when he was already holding me. I anticipated his kiss while he was kissing me. I was overcome by a longing for him so powerful that it distracted me from enjoying the warmth of his hand as we walked together. I used to wish nature would find a way of joining our two bodies even more closely than when we made love. Sure enough, there came a time when I only had to recall his voice to feel him touching me, or his smell to tremble with pleasure. One bright sliver of thought opened my body to love.

The two women continued to strike their faces imploringly, while I was planning to stay at the table. I would lie on it, near the cup. The night was long and the voice of Umm Kulthum would ring out after a while, strong and yet delicate: I would play it to him as he had played it to me. The wailing of the two women engulfed everything in the house, and wound its way in between my clothes and my skin. I would pick up the cup and hold it tight and press it between my breasts.

The Marriage Fair

Almaza worked hard throughout the year for the sake of two and a half days. She devoted all her energy to growing bamboo and weaving it into baskets, only pausing occasionally as she worked to glance at her face in the tin jug that she always had with her. It fulfilled many functions: among other things, she used it for performing the ablutions required by religion, milking the animals and watering the potted plants.

Every time she confronted her reflection in the jug she whispered, "Deliverance is on its way."

The deliverance was the marriage fair: Almaza's whole wardrobe was acquired with this in mind, and all her money earmarked for it. Her tiredness slipped away as she sat with her hands steeped in oil and clay, her hair in rosewater and *ghassoul,* or surrendered her body to the masseuse in the public baths and lay back as the henna artist drew beautiful patterns on her hands and feet. She spent the whole year's savings on her clothes: the straw hat, headcloth and the silver jewelry through her ears and around her head and neck and wrists, the little patterned scarves and the new dress. She didn't forget the incense and perfumed herself with it until it breathed from her eyelashes.

Almaza threw herself into these rituals, which she had perfected instinctively, before setting off for the marriage fair with no inhibitions and no fear of failure, even though she always returned as she had set out, a single woman, unlike her companions, who returned triumphantly with their official promises of marriage, happily discussing their wedding arrangements.

Almaza found herself as usual strolling among the tents where the single men and women gathered, making her way through the sea of penetrating eyes, as prospective husbands studied every eligible young woman, or waited impatiently for the sweethearts they had arranged to meet there: marriages contracted at the fair were lucky, unlike those contracted elsewhere, which were destined to break up.

The marriage fair took place at the same time as a religious festival when many families came to celebrate the memory of a saint buried in the region, and pray for blessings at his tomb and for the warm sun of prosperity to shine on their lives in the coming year. Apart from this there was much fun and entertainment to be had during the three days; the fair included a market selling everything from wheat, barley, animal feed and sugar to luxury goods brought in from the cities.

Almaza never remained with the single women for more than a few minutes. One of the men would pick her out and she would walk with him and sit with him, their hands almost touching. But they never went to have their photograph taken together, like the couples who had decided to marry and rounded off the religious and legal formalities with a visit to the photographer; they never went to put their thumbprints on a wedding document, and Almaza had never worn the black wool cloak striped with red and yellow that her future husband was supposed to give her. She walked back home with the group from her village, alongside laughing women who had won their lifetime's companions and prospective bridegrooms whose chests swelled with pride, all of them thinking about the weddings to come, while she thought about working hard, and preparing herself for next year's fair.

Almaza would cast a last glance over the tents as they were taken down, the revelers and pilgrims gathering their baggage, ready to depart, the vendors loading their unsold goods on to donkeys and camels, and the tears would run down her brown cheeks like little white rabbits. She would murmur to one of the new brides-to-be who was consoling her, "Never mind. God is generous. There'll be another year and another fair."

She knew that she would repeat these words often over the next few days—to her old aunt whom she lived with, to the other old women and young girls in the village and anyone else who noticed that there was no striped woolen cloak around her shoulders. She realized that behind her back they all discussed why she was on the shelf although she was pretty, with a good figure, a beauty spot by her mouth and a nice smile. There were those who believed she had the eyes of a flirt, and men feared a woman who looked as volatile as a hive of discontented bees; others just thought it was her lot in life to remain unmarried.

Almaza could have kept going to the fair year after year, until she was approaching her thirties, and still come back with no woolen cloak, a few more lines on her forehead and whispered comments flying around her ears.

However, this particular year a young man saw her among the hundreds of single women, lost his heart to her and ran after her. But it was the mischievous eyes that had captivated him in the first place, their restless expression throwing him off balance and making him seek refuge in the dark beauty spot on her chin, until that had gathered him up and thrown him into the waves of laughter, which revealed even white teeth like pearls.

Almaza swung her hips gently as she walked with him, and laughed; she was silent or whispered shy words, touched his warm hand, let him put his arm around her and draw her close so that their hips were touching. She listened carefully to all he said, learned his name and what he did, looked at his brown hands and touched them and craved the cigarette he held tightly between his fingers. She asked him for a drag but he offered her a whole cigarette and she puffed on it contentedly.

Nobody looked at them; people were attracted by the crowds in front of them, the market stalls, the sweetmeats, the mothers with their children, while the single men and women were in twos in every corner, leaning against the trees, sitting on the rocks, happily conferring.

After a day and a half, Almaza was turning into a beautiful flower, because of the faint blush always on her cheeks and the fragrance constantly around her; she was a butterfly, tipsy from the excess of the sweet words he spoke to her, a bee drowning in the nectar of intimacy. Nevertheless, on the third day he went away again, and she was left alone with no cloak and no marriage document, to walk home with tears in her eyes. But she was unable to bury the memory of the two and a half days in her usual way, by working, pausing to sigh from time to time, and listening to her aunt shouting that there must be somebody who wished her niece ill, since the young man, who had chosen her and thought she had chosen him, followed her home. He was almost out of his mind because she had cooled toward him when he had tried to take her off to the marriage clerk. He didn't understand her behavior. She had told him during the fair that she was certain to inherit the blood disease that had killed her mother and grandmother, but he had been quick to reply that it didn't matter, he was happy to take the risk.

She had burst into tears at intervals and said it was impossible for them to be together, and he had repeated that he wanted to marry her and would always be by her side. But she had not been convinced. She had asked him to think carefully, not to have any illusions about a houseful of children, rather to prepare himself for a lifetime of sitting in doctors' waiting rooms in the city after a tiring journey over rough mountain roads. His money would go on doctors' bills; she would be cut off in her prime, leaving him with a babe in arms or no heir at all. However, there had not been a flicker of doubt in his eyes; taking her hand and drawing her close, he had assured her of his devotion. When he held her tight, she had burst into tears and finally confessed to him that she had the illness already. Even then he had not flinched; he had continued to breathe evenly and assure her again in a controlled but slightly raised voice that he meant what he said.

While she had composed herself and tried to make him take in what the illness would mean, he had been unable to take his eyes off hers: they were coquettish, tender, sincere, beautiful. When she wiped away her tears, lowering her eyelids for a moment, he had known he had to be at her side always. He had gone on trying to persuade her; she had resisted him, insisting that she was acting out of concern for him.

Eventually he had grown angry and asked her why she had responded to his looks, his gestures if she was unable to marry. Why had she let him hold her hand? Surely she had known that holding hands meant acceptance, covering them refusal? If she had kept her hands covered to prevent him from touching them, he would have gone to look for some-one else.

He had begun to question her relentlessly and Almaza, in floods of tears, had told him why she had given in to him:

love had struck her like the sun flooding over her naked body. She had not been able to escape it: indeed, she had let herself be carried along, enveloped in its heat, from one delicious swoon to another, and had only been roused by him thundering out the conditions for marriage.

Then she had run away from him.

When she saw him coming toward her house she was at a loss and cowered behind her aunt. She pinched the old woman hard so that she would back her up when she told lies, but her aunt cursed her and called her a flea and an armpit louse.

Before Almaza had the chance to work on her further, the young man was standing right inside the house, proclaiming that he had come to marry Almaza, and that illnesses were acts of God, and that in any case he would take her to the city and spend all his savings on finding a cure for her.

During this speech, Almaza had rapidly regained her composure and armed herself with the basic weapons of her defense, chief of which was presence of mind. She began distracting him with details that she knew were unimportant, such as how would she be able to pay him back for the marriage document, the photographs and all the expenses she had involved him in if she were laid low by illness? But she hadn't prepared herself for his reaction. He loosened the sash he wore around his waist and emptied his pockets of old and new notes, scattering them on the ground as if he were feeding hens.

"All this is your dowry for the time being, and there'll be more to come. If we split up, it's yours to keep."

Whereupon Almaza buried her face in her hands and wept and shook her head, disregarding her aunt, who had risen up from her seat on the floor and was crawling around on her hands and knees like an old tortoise, collecting the money, and intoning, "It's not right. Money on the floor is bad luck. It shows ingratitude for God's gifts."

The young man then turned to address the aunt, and told her that he intended to marry Almaza, regardless of her illness. But the aunt insisted that Almaza was no better than an attack of fleas or lice under the arms, an unkind niece whom God had decreed should never marry because she didn't deserve anything good in this world.

He gave up with the aunt, although he couldn't help watching her as she started gathering the money in her skirt as if she were picking fruit. He turned back to Almaza to tell her he had decided to marry her and nothing would make him change his mind. Almaza was silent; she was disillusioned by what was happening to her and gazed abstractedly beyond him. She had expected anything but this from the marriage fair: he hadn't run away like the others, he hadn't flushed or turned pale when she told him about her illness, stuttered with embarrassment, shaken his head regretfully. Instead it was as if she'd opened her arms to him, said she was in the best of health and promised him lots of beautiful children.

He was urging her to say yes, but she said nothing and stared fixedly at the dried cane stalks stacked at the far end of the room, hoping to make him think that her illness was preoccupying her. But she was afraid that her patience was wearing thin and she might blurt out the truth: that he had guessed right and she was not ill but had decided never to get married years before, when she had realized that marriage poured cold water on the excitement and strange, special nature of a relationship, and love froze over. The longed-for, lusted-after sweetheart became the traveling companion who smoothed out the bumpy road, a cow with milk exploding from her udders, a pair of hands to wash the sheets and make the bed ready, not for uninterrupted intimacy, but for sleep as heavy as a temporary death, and a husband snoring after a heavy meal, his sense of smell gone now that he had stopped sniffing out women.

She remembered the second night with her cousin in the tent. She had walked for three days to reach him. She and her mother were supposed to take turns on the donkey, but because her mother had agreed to the difficult journey despite her frail constitution, Almaza insisted that she ride all the time.

The second night he had made sure they were all asleep in their tents, just as he had done the first night, but he hadn't approached her in the same way: she didn't hear the beating of his heart before she felt his hand; he didn't strike his nose with his clenched fist when he saw her breasts, which were permanently in his mouth the second night, except when he snuffled around between them a little, then lifted his head to ask her an irrelevant question.

Almaza forced herself to shake off the images of the tent, to break free from the pervasive odors of her cousin-lover's body, and reimmerse herself in her recollections of the days following the weddings of female relatives and neighbors, when she had been shocked by the way they looked—as if someone had scooped the froth off a drink and left the flat, stale, lifeless liquid. She was shocked too by their empty eyes, which only ever lit up at the sight of their wedding dresses. These outfits reminded them of the days of their engagement, when they were waiting for a new, delightful, unknown page to be turned as they wove the cloth and embroidered it with bright colors. Even this sight lost its appeal as the colors faded, and they were too bowed down by the cares of home and children to look anymore.

The young man was interfering, and drawing her away from these black clouds, wearing down her obstinacy, entreating her to accept. Perhaps she should. Perhaps he wasn't like other men. He had followed her there and he was trying his best to persuade her. But he was raising his voice, declaring that he would marry her even if he had to force her, for she had pulled him halfway out of the well, then cut the rope. His exasperation seemed to be starting to equal his infatuation. He had made up his mind and he wouldn't go back on his decision. He shouted across to her aunt, who was still smoothing out the banknotes as if they were tobacco leaves, and asked her to help him force Almaza to marry him. He wanted to teach her a lesson, so that she wouldn't go playing with fire.

Playing with fire? No, she had been waiting for the fair and preparing her whole being for the sake of this special feeling, this intimacy with an unknown man for two and a half days, so that she could preserve the image and the memories for a whole year, close at hand like winter stores, which she could bring out when she needed them. She could recall the warmth and excitement like a breeze laden with an intoxicating perfume. She could bring back the touching, the whispering, the way they had looked into each other's eyes, or danced, with their shoulders brushing in time to the music. She could remember the music, the food, the noise, the sweets they had bought, and, above all, the men's longing eyes as they followed her, thinking only of the woman, which at that moment was her. They poured out their lives into her eyes, her breasts, her waist, her bottom.

That was the only part she liked: the varying faces, the sinewy hands, not the reality of the characters behind them and the troubles they brought, which were the lightning conductors taking hold of the flash and snuffing it out.

The Land of Dreams

Ingrid cast a glance over the luggage piled up in the hall and hurried off to fetch a scarf to cover her blond hair. After a moment's thought she changed it for another, not because the color didn't match what she was wearing, for she rarely paid attention to her appearance, even at home. It was just that here, she always had to be sure that her clothes were suitable: that they had long sleeves, didn't show her cleavage, didn't cling to her body, and covered her knees.

She settled on the thick scarf to deter stray lice. According to Souad, they adored blond hair for its novelty, and craved the taste of a scalp fragrant with shampoo and clean water, but Ingrid minded more that they were stubborn and vicious and bit through material in search of food, and warmth in winter, or shade in summer, briefly resisting the shampoo especially designed to eliminate them, before succumbing to their fate.

Ingrid sat on the window ledge that she had appropriated as a seat, looking out over her little garden and the road. When her eyes had once more grown accustomed to the wild plants and the dark gray paving stones that had been laid in place of soil, because of sandstorms, she transferred her gaze to the shop across the road, which she had thought was derelict when she first moved into the house. She had even thought Sanaa was an abandoned city as she looked down from the aircraft at the barren mountainsides, the houses scattered over the vast expanses of empty land, and the lookout towers the color of sand. What she saw convinced her that her mission here would be extremely simple. This country appeared to be ideal—virgin territory, not yet visited by people with different religions and world philosophies to debate and defend. But as the aircraft landed, the earth split open and up sprung a city that was a riot of sounds and colors, and of customs she had never encountered before.

Ingrid looked at her watch: Mahyoub was late. Only an hour late; that was nothing. She had grown used to waiting for people for hours. She was even mentally prepared for people not turning up on the right day at all, perhaps even arriving several days later. Time lay like a swamp, and people had stopped winding their watches long ago. This used to annoy her at the start. She had tried to fight it without success, not giving up hope until she had finally acclimatized herself to the way life was here, and begun to understand how a traveler relied on luck to move from one area to another. By that stage she was able to picture the empty, winding roads that appeared to lead only to more dust and more bare hills, and where there was rarely another vehicle in sight. Problems with transportation had themselves played a part in her becoming friendly with Souad, Mahyoub's sister. Ingrid and some other teachers from the school where she taught had set out to visit the village closest to Sanaa as a first step toward discovering what lay beyond the city.

Like the rest of the staff, she had spent the first month after her arrival skating on thin ice, treading on eggshells. When they ventured beyond the protective embrace of the city they felt as if they were at the edge of an abyss and were relieved to encounter two men hitching a lift. As a result they were guided for nothing to the village that was subsequently to become the focus of Ingrid's life and change her from a European woman into one who wore Yemeni clothes, baked bread on an outdoor clay oven, spoke Arabic and hennaed her hands, a custom she was told went back to the Prophet Muhammad, when he wanted to differentiate women's hands from men's.

Ingrid used to notice one particular woman who always came into the shop opposite her home in Sanaa. She began to identify her by the colored cloth bag she carried, as all the older women veiled themselves in an identical fashion: the sheet hanging down either side of the head and the soft black silky material, patterned with red, covering the face. This cloth bag never left the woman's hand. At the beginning Ingrid was certain that she came to beg, as people like her shopped at the local markets, not in these expensive shops, which were patronized mainly by foreigners and government employees. How naive she must have been to believe that this woman was suitable territory in which to sow the first seeds of her mission! She actually went up to her and invited her to her house and the woman went along with her at once, as if she'd been expecting her. Once inside the house she wandered around the room and finally came to a stop in front of the mirror, where she spent some time examining her reflection in amusement. Then she went over and patted the sofa, picked up an ashtray and viewed it from all angles before returning it to the table, stared at the photos of Ingrid's family, and felt the curtains. She went into the bedroom and sat on the bed and bounced up and down like a child. She drank a glass of cold fruit juice in one gulp, and then seemed content to gaze at Ingrid's face, not understanding a word of the other's attempts to talk to her in Arabic. Ingrid was afraid that this opportunity would slip through her fingers and hurried to fetch the woman a picture of the crucified Christ. The woman drew her breath in sharply, putting a hand up to her mouth, but her attention was distracted by the knitted tea cosy. She mumbled a few words and seemed to be asking whether Ingrid had made it and laughed again, pointing at the teapot, apparently finding it strange that it should have a cover at all. Then she smiled broadly at Ingrid, nodded her head as if to say she'd be back again soon, and went out the door. Later Ingrid discovered that she came to the shop only to curse the cigarette display, because her daughter's husband had left her for another woman and he used to buy his cigarettes there. It was then that Ingrid realized that her task was not going to be easy, as she would need excellent Arabic in addition to trying to understand the culture of the country.

Many months had gone by, in the course of which Ingrid believed that she had begun to be able to understand the people's mentality and decipher their behavior. But whenever she went deeper below the surface, she lost her way inside their compact heads, intelligent eyes and smiling mouths.

Mahyoub's car finally came in sight and he drew up and got out, but instead of returning her enthusiastic greeting he stood talking to the owner of the shop. She tried to attract his attention by waving her hands about, but he ignored her until she opened the window and called to him to help her out with some of the luggage.

Usually it was made up of bundles of cuttings from European magazines, small cheap mirrors, paper, pencil stubs, tins of food and packets of cornflakes, but today it included far more important items: a sewing machine, a sterilizer for babies' bottles, boxes of tools, secondhand cooking pots and matches.

When they had finished stowing them in the backseat of the car, which was buckled from a previous accident, Ingrid climbed into the passenger seat. She was worried because she was sure that Mahyoub wouldn't give the load in the back a second thought, but she soon became more concerned about his unsmiling face and abrupt way of talking. The day before, a truck driver from the village had passed on a message from Souad to say that Mahyoub would give Ingrid a lift to the village. This had surprised her, as she hadn't forgotten his hostile attitude toward her the last time she visited them before her trip back to Denmark. She had introduced the head of her school to the men and asked them to invite him to spend a few days there while she was away. They had agreed with a collective nod, their cheeks bulging with qat, all except Mahyoub, who, to her astonishment, had asked why he should be invited. She had grown used to their impeccable hospitality and the way they agreed to all her requests even if they did nothing further to carry them out. She felt herself flushing, but answered: "So that he can get to know you and understand your culture better."

"You mean he's coming to inspect our dandruff and daggers?" he mocked.

Then he had asked why she kept her head covered when she wasn't a Yemeni, or even a Muslim, and held out some qat leaves to her, inviting her derisively to chew qat with them. The other men had silenced him and the oldest man present had risen to his feet in anger, his eyes blazing and threatening violence.

Ingrid felt heavy, as if her luggage in the backseat were weighing her down, making her tongue-tied and even restricting her freedom to breathe. She guessed she felt this way because she couldn't talk to Mahyoub; she wanted to ask him not to drive so fast around bends and not to crowd other cars, but she couldn't even bring herself to ask after his sister and everyone in the village. Her spirits lifted when a haunting song came through the crackle and interference on the car radio but she didn't feel at ease with him like before. Besides looking morose and talking in monosyllables, he drove recklessly and sighed and grumbled and gave her mutinous stares.

Her feeling of awkwardness was justified. After some time, Mahyoub gestured toward her head scarf, saying in bad English, "Either you're bald or your hair's gone gray, Ingrid."

"Maybe," she replied. "And it shows respect."

This time he actually touched her scarf. "You don't have to respect the car," he said, "or me."

And suddenly he was pulling the scarf from her head and allowing her blond hair to fall onto her shoulders. It was thick, and the color of the sun. While she was still recovering from the shock of this unexpected behavior, he shouted, "Now I believe! Glory be to God! Now I believe, Lord!"

She was even more confused, impressed by the emotion and sincerity of his words, yet outraged by his boldness. But she recovered quickly, attributing his behavior to childishness rather than male cunning, and felt justified in this view when he warned her not to let her hair down in front of the village women or they'd be jealous and cut it off while she was asleep.

She tried to divert him, as she had done in the past, by teaching him some English, the language that he saw as a passport to a better life. She asked him to construct sentences with a verb, a subject and an object, using conditional particles, negatives, and past, present and future tenses. This made her feel that she was being useful, but she also derived pleasure and amusement from the examples he gave her, which were at once strange and simple. She remembered some of them: "I will not tell anyone my secret even if my head is separated from my body and my limbs are cut off." "I have an aircraft." And he wouldn't leave that sentence there. The blood had rushed into his face and he had refused to continue the lesson, shouting, "I have an aircraft! I have an aircraft! And yet I let myself rot away here."

But now he wasn't responding to her. He sighed deeply, and she wasn't able to persuade him to become involved in the lesson, or give him advice about his work as a low-grade accountant in an airline company. Not that she had a special interest in him, but she had taken it upon herself to hand out advice to the villagers who had adopted her. She used to urge them not to be satisfied, not to surrender to their fate, repeating, "It is written," but to transcend their circumstances, which means she encouraged secondary-school pupils to go to university and small farmers to grow crops they hadn't tried before.

Mahyoub sighed again and Ingrid guessed he was going to return to the subject of emigrating.

"What's wrong?" she asked finally.

"I don't want to talk about it," he answered.

She didn't ask him what it was that he didn't want to talk about. She knew it was hard for him to earn enough to live on, his prospects of promotion were poor, and he had been waiting for a year for a visa to join a relative in Saudi Arabia.

The car jolted and bounced over the potholes and around the hairpin bends and Ingrid recovered her equilibrium, lost momentarily when her focus on what she represented here, and what she wanted from living here, had been blurred by a trivial gesture toward her hair. Mahyoub's behavior had made her think again and she realized that she had to allow some unspoken complicity to exist between herself and the village. She could not become part of their lives and identify with their particular ways while she remained in their eyes as remote as a heroine from one of their folktales, or a princess imprisoned in a palace that no one could enter. But she said nothing. The days were gone when she used to try and persuade him that he was better off here and should give up his ambitions to go to Europe, and she no longer criticized the men who migrated to Saudi Arabia and left their wives and children for years on end.

She would have loved at that moment to tell him about

her recent experience when she went back home: how all she had thought about was these mountains, this earthly paradise, this secure life, remote from outer and inner turmoil and moral decay. Here it was possible to while away the time without being troubled by modern civilization. Peace of mind existed in these half-empty houses, which contained only mattresses to sleep on, dishes to eat off, a toilet, a lamp. This was paradise.

Ingrid turned toward him calculating whether, if she said this out loud to him, he would fly off the handle, and shout, "What's the point of being in paradise if you don't have enough to eat?"

Or would he nod his head in agreement? "I know. I know. But we have to try the other life. See what it's like working there, then choose."

What? You want to try working over there? Pitiless work which will rob you of your pride as you scrub toilets and sinks, and sweep up the dogshit in public parks, then spend hours purifying yourself from their filth?

Mahyoub was the one man who didn't accept what she said open-mouthed, content merely to stare back at her captivating features like the rest of them. He argued with her and lost his temper, especially on recent occasions, and once, when she was envying them their happy life, he had shouted, "It's all right for you. You'll go home and turn on the hot tap, sleep with your head on a pillow, eat off your individual plate, drink milk and Pepsi from bottles."

Then he had criticized her for not giving the women advice about their medical and social problems. Ingrid had paused to collect her thoughts and laughed a series of short, irritable laughs. "Who am I to tell them to wash their hair?" she had said finally. "I'm here to speak to the mind, the heart. I'm here—"

He had interrupted, his fist clenched: "You're talking to the soul? The mind? While the mosquitoes and bilharzia worms run riot and qat dries up the mothers' milk?"

Something he had said on another occasion had sprung into her head, something quite different: "Qat, Ingrid! God sends it down like manna from heaven. He knows all about our poverty and gives it to us to chew so that we don't want meat and chicken. We chew qat and its bitterness makes us forget the delights of food. Have some. It's fresh. It'll make your eyes shine!"

She hadn't reminded him of this piece of popular wisdom, but answered defensively, "I'm not part of a medical mission, and I don't have the money to improve conditions. I don't work for a government organization. But can't you sense how happy the women are to have me here? Don't you think I'm having some effect on this village? Do you remember when I wanted to revive beekeeping? I went to—"

But he had interrupted her sarcastically: "You talk to the soul? You're so vain! You must be under the illusion that everyone listens to you and believes what you say and acts on your suggestions. Don't you realize that the moment you walk out of the men's sitting room we discuss why you're not married and whether you're still a virgin?"

Ingrid had suddenly felt afraid. Was her relationship with the village so one-sided? It couldn't be. She had tried to convince herself he was sexually frustrated. She had a great relationship with the women, and the men too. When she was away, they all missed her.

Mahyoub stopped sighing and broke the silence, interrupting her internal debate with a blow to the solar plexus. "I didn't think I'd miss you. I felt as if my hand had been cut off. Every couple of days I went down to Sanaa and knocked on your door."

Ingrid attempted a laugh, and tapped him reprovingly on the arm like an older sister. She tried to explain to him that she had become part of his family, but soon lapsed into an uneasy silence. He reached out his hand, imprisoning her hand in his, then turned his face toward her, taking his eyes off the road. "I've fallen in love with you. I can't change that," he said emotionally. "If you turn me down, you'll break my heart."

Her hand fidgeted under his. It was a measure of her rebellion that showed plainly in her eyes, in the reddening of her nose, and the uncomfortable pounding of her heart.

"I want to do it properly, Ingrid, the right way. I want to marry you and have children."

She shuddered. This was what she had feared. He was clinging to her as if she were a life preserver, trying love as a way to escape to Europe. She was like the others, then: like Yvonne, like Ferial, the Turkish girl, whom Ahmad had made a fool of, lavishing words of love on her. They had married and gone abroad and he had disappeared in the airport in Geneva.

One foreign woman here obviously appeared indistinguishable from another. All she amounted to was a passport.

She didn't answer him. She let him talk on in his own language, which she understood fairly well, about the void she had left behind her, how angry he had been with her because she hadn't left her address or phone number, how he had gone to the head of her school, who had claimed not to know them either. He had been scared she wasn't coming back and had thought about finding a way of going to Denmark to look for her.

Ingrid couldn't help responding with scorn: "You know

Denmark well, do you? You'd have stood at the top of a hill and called my name and I'd have come running?"

The sentences flew out as images crowded in on her: when she had gone into the men's sitting room Mahyoub had not shaken her hand. He had ignored her and looked at the school head, Marcel, suspiciously and without warmth. His sister Souad had welcomed her even more eagerly than on previous visits, trying to work out if Marcel was her fiancé.

How could Mahyoub make advances to her now? Abandon his morals and try to seduce her? He wouldn't be able to act like this with a Yemeni woman, or any other Arab woman. The blue of her eyes obviously gave him license to be bold. Too bad. But what if he had known she was a missionary?

Ingrid's eyes were wide and blue, but they filled up at the slightest pretext: a sudden breeze, bright sunlight, onions frying, a tender word. Her small nose was permanently red, but her mouth was impossible to describe. It changed rapidly depending on the situation: shut tight in a smile, pursed as a sign that she was deep in thought, moving all ways as she talked or expressed surprise; and when she threw her head back, laughing uproariously, it was like a cave full of uneven white rocks.

It wasn't her height that distinguished her from the other women as much as her strange coloring. Even the animals in the village were attracted by it. Iftikar swore that her cow never took its eyes off Ingrid and watched her wherever she went, and Husniyya too reported that her chickens were rooted to the spot in Ingrid's presence and the cock crowed at odd times of day.

Ingrid was quite content to have acquired this image and compared it with the other buried inside her, concealed from everyone, even her colleagues at the school: her own image of herself as a Christian missionary. Certainly, she used to tell the men of the village stories from the New Testament and the life of Christ, discussing and comparing those common to the Bible and the Quran, but this was in the context of informing them about all the subjects they were ignorant of: that the earth was a ball floating in space, that man had walked on the moon, that there had been periods of famine in Europe too, and social breakdown, unemployment, housing shortages—even in America itself. She would illustrate this information with pictures from magazines, newspapers and books.

A missionary who danced with the women and had a taste for music, stories and gossip? She never talked to the women about the Bible, as she knew it would be risky for her and them. It was for the men to discuss things with her and then talk to their women.

With those thoughts in mind she began to calm down again, although she was afraid that Mahyoub's confession of love might mean that she had to leave the village, and she desperately needed to belong to this world now she had rejected her world forever. She had cut short her visit to Denmark. The image of the red cup floating in a sea of coffee grains on the Nescafe jar, the thought of which had filled her with nostalgia on her first trip to Yemen, no longer mattered to her. She had discovered back home that she didn't even like the taste of Nescafé anymore, nor the cold, regular rhythm of life, the way people approached their daily lives in an organized fashion, with no place for chance or spontaneity, or a little of the anarchy that acts like a thermometer to show the variations in the soul of a place.

She had missed the dusty road where she lived, the flies that, undeterred by her annoyance, clung to her as if they needed her, the handshake of the owner of the shop opposite, although the same hand had been scooping up olives, cutting cheese, then finding its way to his nose.

When Ingrid saw families out walking on the mountain paths and the rocks with their leopardskin markings, she knew they were getting close. She had learned the colors of the rocks and the rare species of trees by heart. Almost at once children began popping up out of nowhere shouting, "Amina! Amina!" (This was the name they had given her in the village.) The women emerged from their houses like rabbits from their burrows that had smelled a juicy carrot, and when they pulled up Mahyoub presented her with a bouquet of wilting flowers, which included sprigs of qat. They decided to leave most of the luggage in the car until nightfall, fearing that the women would pounce on it, and she got out clutching the flowers, her handbag and a few small carrier bags.

She attempted to kiss all the children who clustered around her calling, "Amina! Amina!" and asked them to run and tell Souad that she'd arrived. "Sweets for the one who gets there first."

Her words acted like a fire spreading through them and they scattered and ran like a herd of brightly colored goats leaping over the bare rocky ground. More children came running from the hillsides and out of the houses. The women were waiting for her beside Souad's house, and a few men stood diffidently to one side. The women kissed her and the men called to her, and in no time the valleys and mountains echoed with the sound of her name, and Ingrid felt like a queen again. The children fingered her dress and handbag, and the plastic carrier bags.

Souad rushed out and threw her arms around Ingrid. She tucked a sprig of basil behind her ear, pushing back her head scarf, and reproaching her nonstop for abandoning them. An old woman tried to make herself heard above the noise: "Fatima's having a baby in hospital."

Finally Souad led Ingrid into the house and the rest of the women followed them into the sitting room, which had whitewashed mud-brick walls and was bare except for a few colored cushions on the floor and a heap of clothes on the broad window ledge. The room became a hive of activity. Souad brought in plates of bread and Iftikar followed with a stainless-steel jug, from which she poured coffee into little cups.

"Did you travel alone?" Souad asked Ingrid. "I'd like to try flying one day."

She flapped her arms up and down like wings, then screamed at the smaller children, who were in the process of running off with the plastic bags. As she snatched the bags away out of sight she turned to Ingrid. "I'll drink my coffee and call you," Ingrid told the children reassuringly. "You count from one to five in English."

The women began talking argumentatively about Ingrid as if she weren't there. One said she was fatter and no longer looked like a camel without a backside because of her height. Another declared that the devil had told her Ingrid was dead. Souad silenced them by remarking jokingly, "And I thought she'd got married! Last time she was here I said to her, 'If you get married, Iftikar and I will deliver your baby.' And she seemed to like the idea."

The old woman cut in: "You and Iftikar? Only the Almighty can deliver babies. And foreigners' wombs have stones in them. She'll be in labor for a year. Their kids have such huge heads."

"Fatima's had four children and they've all died," said Souad, trying to switch the course of the conversation again.

"A child of Amina's wouldn't want to come into the world in one of our houses," said the old woman. "He'd like it better in hospital."

The children came back, having counted to twenty, desperate to know what was in the bags for them. They stood there, their hair matted with dust and the dry air, their feet small and black, their faces marked by the sun, chronic thirst and various skin diseases. The voice of Souad's husband demanding to know why Ingrid hadn't gone in to greet the men mingled with the children's eager cries.

The old woman turned to Ingrid: "You go in to the men! Show off your silky, clean hair to make our men happy! Poor things! Let Abu Muhammad, the blind man, smell it for a minute."

The other women snorted with laughter. Souad gestured warningly at them behind her back and asked Ingrid if she wanted to wash after the journey. She pulled her by the hand toward the bathroom, passing the kitchen, where there was a primus stove and a wicker tray piled with dishes. Ingrid went into the bathroom, which was dark and bare except for a jug and a bowl of stale water.

The air was cooler there because it was tucked away among the other rooms and there was only a very small, high window, or because in a bathroom you face yourself alone and naked. Ingrid rested her head in her hands, trying to put a stop to her conflicting thoughts; she felt as if a football match were being played inside her head. She didn't want to believe that her relationship with the village had come to an end because of Mahyoub's behavior, but she couldn't help thinking that its effects would linger on like a blot of ink spreading out across virgin snow. By the time she came out of the bathroom, she had decided that she was too sensitive, almost neurotic.

She found herself giving in to Souad and entering the men's sitting room, the most beautiful room in the house, because it floated between heaven and earth, thanks to its big windows opening onto the mountains, the cultivated terraces, the clouds and the arid land. The white silken threads of smoke had spun themselves into a cocoon, and the mouthpieces of the narghiles were like colored snakes coiling between the cushions and twisting up into men's hands and between their puckered lips. They chewed qat from the supplies set out before them on the table, and their eyes protruded and swam in and out of focus.

Ingrid went in, and it was unlike any other time. She was as dry as a stick of firewood, and her scarf was tied firmly over her hair. Mahyoub's eyes were like an iron bolt locking her out of the village. She sat down awkwardly and forced a smile in response to their welcoming laughter, trying to control her feelings and behave normally, to be cheerful and tolerant, responding openly to their questions and even their teasing. She began telling them stories, from memory and from the Gospels. Usually they became like children at this point, paying rapt attention and easily affected by what they heard. She had once told them what Jesus said to his disciples in the Garden of Gethsemane a few hours before his crucifixion: "My soul is exceedingly sorrowful, even unto death: tarry ye here and watch with me." And how, instead of comforting him and staying awake with him, they all fell asleep and left him alone.

Said had burst out in anger, "And they call themselves men. They're as spineless as women."

Souad's husband had compared it with the time the Prophet hid in the cave with Abu Bakr, and the dove laid its eggs at the entrance and the spider spun its web.

"But Abu Bakr would have been scared when he heard the sound of the unbelievers' horses," another man had commented, "if the Prophet hadn't reassured him and said, 'Don't be afraid. God is with us.' "

Ingrid's discomfiture was obvious. The men couldn't help noticing it, and whispered to one another that she was no longer with them, and that she must be going to get married in her own country and leave them.

Ingrid steeled herself, and went to play with the children in the women's room. She sat on the floor and made them crowd around her while she distributed pens, exercise books, pictures from European magazines, sweets, chewing gum and toys from the plastic carrier bags, ignoring the women, who had again begun talking about her as if she weren't there and criticizing her for staying away for so many months—half a year, maybe. Ingrid did a quick mental calculation and it was hardly more than a month. Then they began demanding to know if she had got married, given that she had changed so much. "She's drunk our water," said Souad dismissively, "so she'll only be able to marry a man from this village."

Should she get up at this point, and run away from their wagging tongues, or tell them the truth, very calmly, and ask them to stop behaving in this manner, tell them they must understand that there were women who weren't made for marriage and childbirth, and that there was no reason to pity them? But she did nothing of the sort. She was shocked by her rebellious feelings, the simmering tension that made her snatch the sprig of basil from behind her ear and lay it beside her, muttering, "The basil's very strong. It's giving me a headache."

The children's laughter gradually restored her equanimity and she picked up the basil and put it in her lap.

Her eyes looked beyond the door of the room, beyond the countryside that was visible from the window, and she heard a dog howling as if someone was tormenting it. The women's voices seemed to be coming from a distance and the men's voices rumbled up from deep inside a cave.

She sat where she was, refusing to go back into the men's sitting room as she had promised them, even though Souad's husband cleared his throat insistently and spat on the floor outside the women's door. Souad asked her if she was ill. She shook her head. "You must be homesick, then," said Souad.

But Ingrid was thinking of going back to Sanaa. She wanted to be alone to try and resolve her feelings; here she was unable to question them or put a brake on them. They had taken hold of her and were rocking her to and fro until her heart pounded like a church bell. They were like a big clove of garlic that flew out of the mortar when you tried to crush it. She couldn't actually blame Mahyoub for spoiling their friendship and thinking of his own interests, because in a way she had done the same in her dealings with all of them. The thought filled her with anguish and she began reproaching herself: if only she hadn't smiled and laughed and joked so much, this wouldn't have happened. She should have been content to talk to Souad and the other women and build up relationships with them. She shouldn't have let herself get sidetracked when she was telling the story of Mary Magdalene, or Aisha, Mother of the Believers, and the Prophet's wives. If only she hadn't answered . . .

Eventually Ingrid lay down next to Souad, despite these tiresome thoughts, which had kept her up long after Souad had despaired of talking to her till dawn, as they had done in the past, and was fast asleep and snoring. They used to discuss a variety of topics, even though sometimes what each understood was restricted to a few sentences, or a couple of anecdotes. Nevertheless, they had talked on as if talking to themselves.

Ingrid dressed in a leisurely fashion, although Souad had been up for some time. She pulled on her skirt, which she had dropped beside the mattress when she slept, and slipped out onto the balcony. She had been trying not to pay too much attention to the view, in case it was what had made her hurry back to Yemen, but now she couldn't help being transfixed by it: the mist was rising from the mountaintops and floating down into the valleys; the smoke bore the smell of wild plants and wood toward her from the houses, which were like brightly colored cubes scattered over the terraces, and she imagined the fires being lit under the coffee jugs and cooking pots, and in the clay ovens.

Ingrid's eyes alighted on the yard of a house where smoke was rising from the oven and she tried to make out the woman baking bread and preparing breakfast there, marveling at how all the women found time to dress in their finery: loose trousers, dress, cummerbund, necklaces and bright scarves so that they looked like oddly shaped, multicolored flowers. She caught herself peering around for Mahyoub's car. She wanted to send him a message asking him to give her a lift back to Sanaa. When she eventually noticed it, parked under a solitary tree, she thought of going to wake him, then thrust the idea from her mind as if it were infectious, furious with herself for having entertained it at all. She moved away from the window and paced around the room. But had she not gone to his house before, when Souad was ill, and almost dragged him out of bed?

Ingrid had been on her second visit to the village, invited by Souad, whom she had just met. Souad's warm smile and overwhelming generosity had been hard to resist, but she was also encouraged by the fact that Souad's husband was away in Saudi Arabia at the time. As soon as she got out of the car, which had brought her all the way from Sanaa, the children crowded around her, repeating Souad's name. She nodded her head, smiling with pleasure at the welcome. She didn't pick up on the anxiety and tension in the words and faces, nor understand what it meant when a woman came running and pointing to Souad's house and repeating Souad's name within earshot of the driver of the foreign mission's car. But neither Ingrid nor the driver understood and Ingrid took it to be a further expression of welcome, until she finally went into Souad's house and found her in bed under piles of her own and the neighbors' clothes, although at that time of year the heat rose up and hit you, even from the cracks in the walls. Souad wasn't moving except to throw up helplessly, having given up hope of controlling her diarrhea. Ingrid understood from the women who were sitting dejectedly around her, taking turns putting hot vinegar poultices on her forehead, that she had been like this for several days. Ingrid hurried out onto the porch and saw the mission car disappearing down the winding mountain road, reduced to the size of a small insect. She looked around her, unable to believe that there was nothing she could do but sit there like the grim-faced women around Souad. She went inside and asked if there was a telephone anywhere nearby, then went back outside and looked in despair and disbelief at the emptiness, overcome by a feeling of loathing for this silent countryside. Suddenly she noticed a car parked down the valley beside a house. She stared hard and rubbed her eyes, as they say in stories. She rushed back in, gesturing toward the car, praying that they wouldn't tell her it had broken down. The women gathered around her and began shaking their heads disapprovingly, and one of them spat on the floor. Finally Ingrid understood that the car belonged to Mahyoub, Souad's brother. She tried to find out why nobody had thought of turning to him for help, but was irritated by them talking all at once in loud voices and beating their breasts, and hurried out to find some children to go and fetch him.

Ingrid imagined that Mahyoub would come rushing

over, but the children returned, saying he was asleep and didn't want to wake up. Ingrid flushed bright red and, seething with rage, she was off, almost hurling herself down the moutainside, slipping and sliding over the rocks and stones, surrounded by children whose shouting made the women they passed look up from their baking or washing.

She found herself in the middle of a room made bright with cheap rugs on the walls and floor, curtains at the windows and cushions and backrests around the sides. One huddled mass of color moved and sat up. She told him in English that Souad was nearly dying of dehydration and that they must get her to the hospital.

She couldn't believe the cool indifference in his voice. He told her that Souad wasn't strong enough to walk and that it would be difficult to carry her down in her condition as her house had been built at the top of the mountain and it was a fair climb to reach it. Ingrid wondered if he was still half asleep, or didn't understand the gravity of his sister's condition. She explained the position to him slowly and deliberately, and Mahyoub repeated what he had already said to her, also slowly and deliberately, and was clearly wide awake.

"What will you tell her husband if your sister dies?" shouted Ingrid. "How will you be able to show your face around here? What will you say to people? 'My sister's house was on top of the mountain. It was a difficult climb, and her husband was away'?"

Mahyoub had finally given in, climbed out of bed and gone to call the men to help him get Souad. They wrapped her in a blanket and took her off to the hospital. Ingrid understood from the episode that if the sick person was a woman it mattered less if she lived or died. She still remembered visiting a graveyard and noticing that women had one headstone and men two, but even though she recognized that life was harsh here, she had never managed to understand Mahyoub's behavior toward his sister. The resemblance between the two had startled her, especially when Mahyoub covered his head, which made him look as if he had stepped straight out of a storybook. His head was flat from behind as a result of being swaddled so tightly as a newborn baby, and his features were delicate: he had small eyes like two black pearls, and a short, firm nose; he was slenderly built and had short fingers, which looked as if they had been melted down with use. He parted his curly hair to one side and smothered it in Brylcreem. He was proud of his hairstyle and when Ingrid asked him why he put Brylcreem on it he merely glanced in the car mirror and slicked it down. He was the only man who didn't spit in front of her to moisten his mouth when the qat had made it dry.

Ingrid tried not to let Souad, so eager for information, know what kind of state she was in. But how could she hide her annoyance, which always attacked her throat and chest in the form of red blotches, when she was up against Souad's ultrasensitive radar system? Souad could pick up little wandering veins in the eyes, faint lines contracting the forehead, a slight, tense clenching of the fingers, and above all the inflection of the voice: did it fall gently on the ear, or lacerate the eardrum? Was the mouth slack when chewing food or properly closed? Were there signs of frequent swallowing of saliva?

Ingrid thought up a number of reasons why she had to go back to Sanaa: she said the water seller might have forgotten to turn off the tap on his tanker as usual and her garden would be flooded. "That would be a blessing," said Souad. "The whole quarter would soak up the water and pray for health and plenty for you and your family."

Next Ingrid gasped and said she had some homework to correct in Sanaa.

"I've seen you go through a pile of exercise books like sheep through clover," said Souad.

She seized Ingrid's hand suddenly and turned it over and kissed the palm and the tips of the fingers with her piercing eyes closed. Her skin was golden brown and smooth like apricots. She leapt to her feet, full of energy and sharp intelligence once more. "Let's have coffee and I'll read the cup for you."

She ignored Ingrid's refusal and when she had poured the coffee she held the cup to Ingrid's mouth. When Ingrid still refused to drink it, Souad tipped the coffee back into the jug and began moving the cup around and reading the grounds. "There's a man standing here, saying something. It must be Mahyoub proposing to you."

Before Ingrid could digest this surprise Souad launched into an emotional speech that made Ingrid feel embarrassed as well as increasingly irritated. Souad accompanied her tirade with expressive head and hand movements, and her long silver earrings also played their part. Ingrid didn't understand every sentence, but deduced that Souad was saying that Mahyoub loved her and that while she was away he had fallen ill and turned the color of turmeric and weighed as little as a baby.

Ingrid shook her head and said nothing, but she felt somewhat mollified. Mahyoub must have been sincere and she wasn't merely a way out to Europe for him. But Souad was demanding to know immediately if she would marry Mahyoub to relieve her of the burden her mother had placed on her. She had been left in charge of Mahyoub and she wanted her mother's bones to rest in peace now instead of being curled up in a tense ball, rattling and shaking, while Mahyoub walked this earth alone with no companion to bring him tea and coffee and wish him good morning at daybreak.

"But why me?" Ingrid repeated at intervals throughout Souad's outburst, throwing small stones into the oncoming deluge with no effect. Finally she shouted at the top of her voice, drowning out Souad, "Why me? Why me?"

Without missing a beat Souad answered that it was because she was educated. She could read and write, and no Yemeni girl would be acceptable to Mahyoub because an educated Yemeni girl would demand a high bride price and on top of that would not expect to run a house and work and save. Then she took Ingrid by the hand and said, "You learn fast. You can bake bread in the oven, bless you, even though you burned it a few times, and you help me with the housework. Anyone would think you were born in these parts if it wasn't for all the reading and writing you do."

While Ingrid was looking for the right words to make it clear that there was absolutely no room for maneuver, without causing offense, Souad seized her hand again and kissed it first on one side, then on the other, like a butterfly uncertain where to alight. Then she tried to unfasten her necklace of cornelians with an English gold sovereign in the middle. She asked Ingrid to help, and Ingrid was on the point of obliging when she suddenly realized what the gesture meant—it was the giving gesture. If she refused some particular dish on a social occasion, the lady of the house would be sure to present it to her on her way out. Or if, for example, she admired a woven wicker tray hanging on the wall, or even just asked what it was, her hostess would snatch it down and present it to her. So now Souad was giving her the most precious thing she owned as a pledge of her affection. She tried to explain to her that she had no thoughts of marriage, and if she had she wouldn't do it like this, and anyway she thought of Mahyoub as a brother. But Souad wasn't listening. She was still in full flood, talking of Mahyoub and Mahyoub's heart until her eyes filled with tears and she began sobbing. Ingrid found herself shaking her, and she must have been doing it quite hard, as Souad suddenly went rigid; she hadn't expected this behavior from Ingrid, who was so calm and controlled. But she didn't pay any attention to what Ingrid was saying, since she had convinced herself in advance that she was going to persuade Ingrid to marry her brother, Ingrid who was good-hearted "to the point of naivete sometimes," as people had been known to remark, taking every word anybody said to her seriously. So she recharged her speech with images to set the stream of words in motion again: "If you ascend to heaven and descend into the bowels of the earth, you'll never find anyone who loves you like this. Foreign men have blond hair and light eyes like you, and you'll always be in competition with other women for them."

Souad stopped, struck by what she had just said, and turned her face to Ingrid with a big smile, then went on as if she were talking to herself: "They'll come to us from the villages around about to look at you. You'll become a famous sight: we'll defeat our enemies and silence our critics the moment you let down your blond hair in front of them, and Mahyoub will be the most important person in the village. Women will come from all over the place to ask your advice about health problems or just to sit with you. They'll give you all the best qat."

Ingrid smiled back and let Souad chatter on. She was surprised how calm she felt all of a sudden. Souad talked away, repeating herself to make sure Ingrid hadn't missed anything; it seemed that what Ingrid had said about not getting married now or in the future because she felt that the whole world was her family was of no concern to Souad. The older men whom Ingrid saw as fathers, the younger men who were her brothers, and her children, her mothers and her sisters all evaporated around the room like soap bubbles. She decided to return to Sanaa as soon as she could. The sense of harmony, which used to descend on her the moment she took off her shoes and sat on the floor with the village women, had vanished completely. Now she wanted to sit alone, looking down on her garden in Sanaa until the buzzing and jostling of her thoughts had abated.

She actually left the village with Mahyoub, as Souad

insisted that he should take her, rather than the truck driver who made strangers pay a fare. Souad literally pushed her into Mahyoub's car and he didn't open his mouth all the way, which made things awkward, for she had never wanted a war between them. She tried to start up a conversation, but the only sound that came from him was his heavy, uneasy breathing.

Ingrid sat on her chair in her house in Sanaa looking out over the road and sand and nothingness. When she had been sitting there for some time, she began to grow restless, for her head refused to clear; if anything, the turmoil in her mind increased, especially when she recalled the oppressive atmosphere in the car on the way back and Mahyoub's sullen expression implying that it was all her fault, that she was evil, and dangled the keys to others' happiness under their noses but never opened the doors for them. Ingrid had never been so unsure of herself before, or felt so weak. She almost felt that she had reached the end of her resources. She realized now that she had never experienced the kind of desperation that was so deep rooted in the hearts of those whom she had instructed to be patient in the face of adversity.

She remembered the camel she had gone to visit who was supposed to live in an ancient cave at the heart of the Sanaa market. She couldn't find it and asked a man sitting among sacks of wheat by the flour mill if he knew where the camel was. Realizing that she was foreign, the man had gone through a pantomime for her, tilting his head to one side, then resting it in his palm, before repeating, "He's asleep. Tired." He pointed to the mill. "He works the wheel. Now he's tired. Very tired."

She asked him why he didn't change the camel for another. "He'd die if he didn't work," laughed the man. "He loves working. I blindfold him so he doesn't get dizzy. So that he thinks he's dreaming that he's walking around. He works and sleeps. Sleeps and works."

The image of the camel working and sleeping, sleeping and working, at his own speed, and the mill turning in a cave that was over four hundred years old gave her a feeling of calm, and she paced around in a circle like the camel with her eyes closed, trying to free her head of the tangle of confusion that reminded her of a heap of wires and cables she had seen lying in the street outside. Eventually she recovered her composure, holding tight to what she knew would unravel the tangle: facing up to the truth fairly and squarely. That was always the most important thing, the starting point for being honest with oneself. Only in the presence of honesty did the false pretexts collapse and everything appear convincing and as if it were spread out on a table, accessible to the hand and eye. She was to blame, and Mahyoub and Souad were right: she had behaved like the sun when it winks its eye for a moment and then vanishes behind the clouds, reappearing for a little while, then veiling itself again by degrees, leaving a feeble light that only serves to draw attention to its absence. That was how she had been with them: insincere and cajoling. She had been afraid to show them what she wanted from them, in case she alienated them and her work faltered; then her visits would have come to an end and her conversations with them have served only to furnish material for village gossip. Gradually her anger turned into affection and understanding. She wanted to ask their forgiveness. She missed them and felt lost away from the village.

She rushed into her bedroom and knelt in front of the picture of the Virgin Mary as she had done when she first arrived; all those months ago she had asked her for forgiveness because she couldn't reveal the truth, otherwise her mission would become impossible.

Ingrid was sitting in Souad's room among the village women, who were packed together like kebabs on skewers made up of meat and vegetables of all shapes and sizes and colors. She looked different too, although she had tried her hardest to make them leave her alone. It was as if, despite all her efforts, she'd only touched the surface of the water and it had gone a little cloudy then reverted to normal.

As soon as Souad had announced the wedding, Ingrid had found herself sitting on cushions on the floor stretching out her hands and feet among the henna fumes, while the henna artist bent over them with a matchstick dipped in henna and drew beautiful delicate patterns. Ingrid had to stay awake all night to let them dry and make sure she didn't smudge the fine lines. The next day she dressed in Souad's wedding dress, which had been stored in a cloth bag. The women had insisted that she wear her hair loose. It almost reached her waist and had been covered up for so much of the time that it had grown streaky. The woman who had come to prepare her for the wedding had massaged it for ages, praising its length and thickness to the village women, who were seeing it for the first time and muttered, "In the name of God" as they touched it.

"A moon on two legs," said Iftikar. She recounted how her brother had vowed he would never marry until he had found a fair-haired bride and how she had visited all the girls' schools in the area pretending to be a government employee until she had found a suitable candidate.

"Her hair's dyed," screamed Kawkab. "There's no such thing as a blond Yemeni."

Iftikar swore by all the saints that her sister-in-law was a genuine blonde and threatened to storm out when they disbelieved her, but Souad begged her not to spoil the wedding preparations.

The women couldn't let this occasion go by without expressing to Ingrid the thoughts that raged in their hearts.

"You've abstained for so long," said one. "And now you're marrying a Yemeni. Don't you know Yemeni men are mad?"

She waggled her head about and made her eyes bulge and stuck out her tongue.

"Listen, Amina," advised another. "Have four children, then lock it up," pointing between her legs, "and hide the key."

"Hide it?" cried Iftikar. "You need to lock it and throw away the key, like I did."

They placed the bridal crown on Ingrid's head. It was made of brightly colored cloth. They perfumed her with musk and burned incense around her, then sat her on a high pile of mattresses. These activities were accompanied by waves of song as the women crowded around her and sang to the beat of the drum and the drummer's song: "O bride, beautiful as the moon."

Ingrid sat there, secure in her belief that this was what the Virgin Mary wanted from her. It was amazing how events had unfolded to produce just the right result. She was becoming one of them and so belief in her and consequently in Jesus would automatically pervade their hearts; even without them being aware of it, it would be happening all the time with every glance, every word. She was like a contagious disease, spreading her belief in Jesus among them whether they wanted it or not. Her silent prayers would have their effect on places, faces, souls, especially as she had not been forced to give up her religion and embrace theirs.

Her dialogue with them would never be ended, that was the main thing. Her previous visits had been like a sudden cloudburst: they had gathered around in amazement to watch, but as soon as the rain stopped, off they went back to their normal lives, which revolved around cracking jokes, chewing qat, and discussing politics and the pros and cons of leaving the country in search of work.

Ingrid felt a peace of mind she had never known before. She was so happy she could have flown. What she had achieved, without being fully aware of what she was doing, had in retrospect taken on an irresistible allure, like a miracle. She had traveled through mists and across seas to this remote spot, following a vision that had come to her one evening. A voice had called, "Ingrid! Get up off your knees! These prayers of yours are no longer enough. Go to the ends of the earth, to a land where they haven't seen me. Lift the darkness from their eyes. Tell them about me, then let them choose."

The night Ingrid had decided to marry Mahyoub she had thrown herself down in front of the picture of the Virgin Mary, telling her what had happened, asking for her advice and confessing that she was in love with Mahyoub too. And lo and behold, the Virgin's eyes had signaled their agreement.

The singing and dancing continued while in the kitchen Souad was mixing water with the Pepsi Mahyoub had bought. She was happy because the young woman with blue eyes who saw the world as she saw it with her brown eyes was going to be close at hand forever. Souad was distracted briefly as she wondered if Ingrid remembered the bet, even though it had been made in fun. Souad and the men had realized since the second visit that Ingrid was intending to spread her religion in the area, and the men had decided among themselves not to receive her in case the mere fact of listening to what she had to say interfered with their faith. Souad had nearly gone out of her mind at the thought that the happiness and anticipation she felt at Ingrid's forthcoming visit might be snatched away, and they far surpassed the excitement generated by any village wedding or funeral. It was as if a breath of air from the world she saw sometimes on her brother's television had materialized into a living being and prostrated itself before her, ready to do her bidding.

Souad had therefore taken bets with the men that in the

end Ingrid would become one of them, just as she was in the process of doing now in the room next door.

Nobody apart from Souad believed, or even hoped, that this miracle would come to pass except Mahyoub, and that was because he had been head over heels in love with Ingrid since the moment he first saw her.

Souad finished making the drinks and decided that she would not remind Ingrid of the bet until she had been married for a while, or perhaps she never would. But she couldn't forget the occasion when she had first told Ingrid's fortune in her coffee grounds: "You'll marry one of us and forget your ideas and your stories."

Ingrid had shaken her head, laughing: "Never. I shall never marry and that's definite."

And Souad had taken Ingrid's hand and said, "You will get married, and you'll marry a man from this village. I'll bet my life on it."

Place de la Catastrophe

The woman whom I was used to fleeing with from place to place was lying looking up at me, unable to believe what was happening to me. For the first time since we had met several years before, we knew that our lovemaking would not be abruptly halted, and yet she could feel me freezing on top of her.

"Did you hear something?"

Our ears would have to accustom themselves to disregarding what they heard, for together we had become over-sensitive to any noise, and I don't mean my wife causing a commotion, or someone shouting outside, or a car stopping suddenly, or even laughter floating through an open window: we jumped if the breeze lifted the light curtain, or if either of us took an unexpected breath.

Once we had become tranquil again we would retrieve the feeling of heat that we had left hanging in the air and down around the lower parts of our bodies and become reabsorbed in it, oblivious to everything. Because of the atmosphere of panic and guilt, our bodies were like empty rooms, waiting to be filled quickly, while our minds rushed to keep pace with this thirst, amazed at the strange and wonderful scenes that came crowding into them. We used to exchange these images afterward when our hearts were still beating and our loins throbbing, as they take longer to subside and become ordinary bits of the body again, like a hand or a lock of hair. The woman recounted that she had seen herself sliding over a waterfall and I said I had been a juggler in a circus. Then she whispered that she had seen the branches of a banana tree entering her, and I told her that I had been opening a basket and shutting it again, opening it and shutting it.

I still don't know whether we saw these images because we were being pursued by my wife, nor have I ever understood how she always guessed where we were. Every time she forgave me once again, she would say without affectation, in a voice full of pain, "My misery led me to you."

I would look at her, trying to decide whether she was a prophet or a devil. I couldn't believe that misery never lost its way around the winding roads, disappeared into the valleys, or got caught on a cactus plant. When she tracked me down, she cursed, shouted, wept, mewed like a cat, howled like a dog, reinforcing this barrage of sounds with kicks to hotel room doors, my car, the woman's car, hired cars. She had developed a huge voice with thick roots reaching deep inside her, and she seemed to use it to pick up a place and shake it, and shake the bed we were lying on. I would clench my fists in rage, resolved not to mend my ways, but to create a hideaway that nobody would be able to find. Nevertheless, charged up with anger and uncertainty, I would mount the woman as if she were a mare I had long been deprived of. She therefore became absolutely convinced that my desire for her was the result of a game being played by me and my wife, and that she had fallen into our trap; I left signs and markers for my wife on purpose—if not, how could I explain my short bursts of wild excitement after she had caught us, at a time when her desire had temporarily abandoned her? She tried to persuade me of the truth of her theory without success. Recalling conversations with my wife, I was sure that I had not left any signs, other than telling her that I had an inexplicable passion for this woman's body that didn't interfere with my love for her. I swore to my wife that I had never kissed the woman's hand, nor held her gently in my arms, or passed my finger over her lips, and my conversations with her were limited to details about the color of flesh, pores, pubic hair, or expressions of purely physical ecstasy. My wife covered her ears at my declaration of love. She pulled her hair and slapped me and shook me, as if she hoped my heart would jump out into her hand.

After that she had cosmetic surgery to make her breasts the shape of brandy glasses. She did exercises religiously until her stomach was flat. She wore an endless variety of nightdresses which were made of such fine silk that they were almost illusory. She tried to establish a relationship with my genitals that had nothing to do with me. But they always became cerebral and refused to let her play with them, leaving the talking to me, so that I had to assure her as kindly as I could, and lightheartedly, to dispel her feelings of loneliness, that she had become a part of me.

Now the woman was trying to regain my interest, moving in a way that was unfamiliar to me, but which exuded desire, while I wondered why I had come here when we no longer had to hide. Why was the square where the hotel was situated called Place de la Catastrophe and what exactly was the disaster that had given it its name? It really didn't go with the little houses there, in their tangle of tree branches and brightly colored climbing plants, or the washing spread out to dry on the balconies and the narrow bridge that linked the houses together.

I closed my eyes, urging myself to reach the end of the bridge, to remember what happened when I was inside her. But I couldn't go any farther.

I felt as if there was somebody behind me, coming between me and her, distancing me from her hands clinging to my back. I looked around and the room was peaceful. I told myself I was imagining things and that this was the first time after . . .

But I heard a faint kicking, a feeble mewing. Anxiously, I turned around again, but when I saw that the urn on the dressing table was still I relaxed, determined to give my full attention to the woman, whose legs and arms continued to be wrapped tightly around me. However, the kicking grew stronger, the mewing louder and my car horn gave a shrill blast. I jumped to my feet in a panic. This must all be coming from the urn, my wife's new home. She had insisted that she wanted to be cremated, not buried, when she died, and had begged me never to leave her alone. I had promised at the time, placating her, weeping at the pain which was eating away at her, that I would never leave her for a moment and would take her with me wherever I went. I saw the urn kick the table and was wary of the feet inside it. I heard the mewing and shrieking and was convinced the voice had put down its roots there, and when I involuntarily hid my face in my hands I was certain her eyes were watching too.

I Don't Want to Grow Up

Living in an oil company compound in the middle of the desert, we needed to see a color that was different from the color of the sand, to touch something other than the layer of dust on everything, to enjoy a sound that wasn't the wind, the air conditioner or the chatter of other children. One day our servant, Bus, brought us the thing we longed for without knowing it, or at least he brought it to my little brother. Although I was glad myself, I wondered if Bus's plan was to find another way of being close to my brother, and I began to feel suspicious. His hands were all over him, touching his shoulders, his neck, his face and playing with his hair, and I thought of the Indian goddess with many hands. He wanted me to think he was being fatherly when he adjusted the towel around my brother's waist, but watching him, I decided that he was keen to see him in his bathing trunks. He insisted on having my brother on his lap when he was showing him how to steer a bike or car. Sometimes he would tell him he had a present for him in the pocket of his apron and I would watch my little brother's fingers reaching into the pocket in search of a bar of chocolate or a toy car.

I knew boys had to be careful as well as girls. The boys at school exchanged stories about "perversions" and repeated their parents' warnings to watch out for strangers, but to be especially on their guard against the male servants who almost lived in the houses where they worked. Although I looked up what *perversion* meant in the dictionary, my mind registered the word differently after I had seen photos of two men embracing in a magazine my mother received by post at the beginning of every month. This magazine, which was as thick as a book, rarely contained pictures and when it did they were usually vague black-and-white drawings that didn't mean a thing to me. I revealed my misgivings about Bus to my brother, who was five years younger than me, and fetched my mother's magazine to help him understand. As I showed him the photos, I felt he wasn't taking it in, and sure enough he said, "But Bus doesn't look like either of those men."

Bus was about my height, and very skinny, and if it hadn't been for his wrinkled forehead and gold teeth, he would have looked younger than his years; the two men embracing, on the other hand, were handsome and as tall as bamboo plants, passionately intertwined. They were both dressed in formal suits and ties, like two presidents.

"They must be crying," said my brother. "Maybe one of them's mother died, or his dog."

I sighed in exasperation and showed him another photo. Their faces were touching and they were looking into each other's eyes with love and tenderness like a man and woman in a film.

"Do you see?" I egged him on, pointing at their faces. "Do you understand what I mean?"

But my brother's eager answer fell on me like a cold shower. "Is it a doctor looking at someone's eyes?"

I threw the magazine aside and pointed a warning finger at him, and told him that if Bus touched him on any part of his body, he would be in agony and might even die.

From that moment on my little brother went to great lengths to avoid Bus: he wouldn't meet his eye and refused to stay alone in the same room as him, especially at night when our parents went to visit friends and Bus babysat for us. My little brother clung to my side while we watched television and ate our supper and when I went to the toilet he came too. This annoyed me as I couldn't go with him there even if he turned his face away and looked at the door.

It never occurred to me to reveal my doubts to my mother, even before Bus arrived with the thing that changed our lives. He cut the potatoes in the shape of pears, was an expert at making birthday cakes, helped me color in maps, drew faces like a professional artist, embroidered cherries on my blouse, and besides, I knew how much my mother depended on him. She hardly did a thing in the house, and sat looking at books all day. How then could I ever have complained about him once he had brought the rabbit?

It was a white rabbit like a ball of wool. He built it a hutch and we played with it after school every day and put it back in the hutch before we went to bed. It learned to bang against the door with its forelegs to make us open it. Being an intelligent rabbit, it knew that life was more interesting outside the cage than inside. We let it wander around the house and I followed it, picking up the black pearls it left behind so that my mother wouldn't find them, and shooing it away from her plants. Once it was too quick for me and gobbled half a leaf. It became part of the family, until one evening Bus picked it up by the ears, despite my brother's protests, and said he'd never in all his life seen a rabbit grow so fast, and praised us for our efforts. It was true that we'd stolen extra rations of carrots and lettuce for it behind my mother's back. To our astonishment Bus dropped the rabbit into a basket with a lid that he usually kept fixed to the back of his bike, saying that he wanted to mate it with another rabbit. My brother let out a shriek, not understanding what Bus meant, but Bus immediately pulled out another, smaller rabbit from the basket. My brother only hesitated a few moments before transferring his affection from the old, familiar rabbit to the new, little one.

So it was that as one rabbit grew up Bus exchanged it for another, younger one. My brother got used to this process. Perhaps he even welcomed it, as all rabbits look alike and behave in the same way, from the quivering of their mouths and noses to the expressions in their eyes, but baby rabbits have a particular charm that is hard to resist.

Spring had come and the heat was still bearable. We moved the rabbit hutch out onto the roof, and as we climbed the steps to see it the following morning my brother predicted that the rabbit would be gone.

We had been made to move it, as my mother began to find the smell of rabbits in the hall and kitchen unbearable. She had never let us put it in the garden from the beginning, claiming that she had heard or read that the smell attracted snakes and scorpions.

My brother asked once again if snakes could climb vertically and I assured him that they couldn't and we finally reached the roof terrace. To my surprise, he had guessed right and the rabbit was nowhere to be seen. We stood looking around us uncertainly, until we noticed some movement in a pile of leaves and an old pullover that I'd left up there ages before. It was the withdrawn rabbit, which had never let us play with it like the other rabbits. I managed to separate it from the little creatures it was protecting with its fur. They looked like mice or rats. We picked them up and hurried to show them to Bus, who told us angrily that they'd all die if we separated them from their mother so early on. Sure enough, they all died even though we put them in a cardboard box in the living room with a glass of hot water beside them to give them warmth. When Bus wanted to take them away, we were convinced he wouldn't bury them but would just throw them out with the garbage. So we waited until my father came home from work and took us to bury them outside the compound, where they wouldn't attract snakes to the house, to keep my mother quiet.

As I scrabbled in the sand, I was filled with a kind of happiness, as if I were at the seaside and all that was missing was the sound of the waves breaking on the shore, and the smell of the ocean. It was early evening and from where we were the compound looked like a green dot on a brown paper bag.

We stopped ourselves from picking up the black rabbit and made do with watching its stomach swell. Whenever my brother complained to me, I encouraged him by reminding him of the baby rabbits that would soon be born. Then we discussed whether Bus was going to let us have them all. But he left us one rabbit only, which soon died. We blamed him, claiming that the rabbit had died of grief because it was separated from its brothers and sisters. But Bus laughed scornfully and told us that feeding it parsley and coriander was what had killed it. He promised to bring us another rabbit the next morning.

My brother, pacified, nodded and went out to play, but a few minutes later he rushed back in to tell me that the neighbor's children had a peacock and a bird like a parrot with an electronic voice. I went outside, holding his hand, to ask the children how the peacock and the parrot had got here, and they swore that their servant, Kameel, had brought them from his country.

The compound children had begun to raise young rabbits like us, and their servants, like Bus, would exchange them for younger ones when they grew up. I thought of the canary in a cage that we had seen sitting on the conveyor belt at the airport. The people waiting for their luggage had laughed out loud at the sight of the canary among the suitcases, apparently enjoying the occasion.

One of the children said that peacocks spread their tails out like fans.

"So what, if we can't even see our peacock yet," said another.

I asked him what he meant and they all chorused back at me, "Kameel always forgets to bring it from his room, even though we remind him every day."

"He must be lying," I said. "Bus used to tell my brother that in his country there were TV sets as big as whole rooms."

I decided to take them to the servants' quarters at the far end of the compound. "Why don't we go and find out the truth?" I said.

The children reacted enthusiastically to my suggestion and rushed off like gazelles to ask their parents.

Perhaps they were slow to come back, or was that just how it seemed to me? I took my brother's hand and began running in the direction of the servants' rooms. As I ran, I wondered why I was more anxious than them to see the peacock, or else to find out that the servant had been lying. Why hadn't I grown up yet? I was interested in the rabbits and everything else that filled the days of the younger children, so much so that my mother had told me reprovingly that my brother was more mature than me: this was when I put war paint on the children's faces with felt-tipped pens and it took two days of rubbing with soap and face cream to get it off.

I used to enjoy playing with them, and it made me laugh when they laughed. I was also their leader, teaching them to do dangerous things and suggesting roles for them to act. My cousin, who had stayed in Lebanon and was the same age as me, wrote me letters about boys and makeup and rock singers.

I felt happy, as if I was setting off on an adventure, when the stars came close to the earth and the houses thinned out. The sun was red and almost sinking into the sand, and the twilight turned violet and orange and then gray. I had an idea about the sort of places the compound's servants lived in, because I had always thought of the compound as being like a factory and the servants as the machinery that made it run. They lived near a small mosque whose walls were covered in blue mosaic tiles.

The sense of being my own mistress and having my brother under my control was short-lived as he began lagging behind and complaining that he was tired. When I offered to carry him he confessed that he was scared more than tired; I wondered why, as it never got properly dark in the desert. I looked around for a stone or a stick to defend him with. Everything was still: the gardens were semi-arid and the sloping ground around us was bare except for some fanlike shrubs and a little plant that wilted and surrendered to me, roots and all, the minute I touched it. I gave up the idea of finding a stick or a stone and asked my brother what he was afraid of.

"Bus," he replied.

"Sweetheart," I said, bending down to him. I took him in my arms but changed my mind rapidly when I found how heavy he was, and put him down again.

"Don't be scared. Bus is still in our house. And anyway, you can't be scared when I'm with you!"

I was sorry I had made him frightened of Bus. It reminded me of my grandmother telling me stories about the ghoul to frighten me into being good.

"Why didn't we wait for the others?" he asked. "Why don't we go back and get them?"

"If we go by ourselves, we can see the peacock before they do, and maybe take the bird with the electronic voice," I answered.

"Steal it?"

"Maybe."

I couldn't imagine that there was a peacock or a bird like a parrot in those wooden huts; however, I wanted to escape from the house and also prove that the servant had lied. Darkness enveloped us suddenly, as I had taken a short cut off the main road; then it was gone again as we walked along another road with houses and streetlights on either side.

My brother no longer clung to me. We got nearer and smelled cooking and then heard children talking in a foreign language, and I was sure that they must be the servants' children visiting for the holidays. I had once heard Bus saying that he would have liked to send for his children if the fares hadn't been so high. Hearing other children made us feel easier, but then a man came out of the wooden huts and noticed us and stopped and stared and my heart beat faster again. I knew I must ask him where Bus lived, or Kameel, in the strongest voice I could manage. He indicated the last hut. I thanked him loudly and he went on staring at me. He started to move. Was he going to follow us? My brother was clinging to me so tightly now that I could hardly walk. I realized our parents had been right to be worried: here I was rushing into the trap, and I only understood how terrified my brother was of Bus now that I felt the same way about this man.

A horrible smell distracted my attention, then a washing line strung between the building and the streetlight. We had to duck our heads down under the washing to get to the house the man had indicated. I thought the compound's sewage pipes must come out here. The washing flapped noisily against the back of my head. It seemed strange. They must have used a powder that made their clothes dry hard and stiff in the sun. The smell grew stronger and the washing was all the same shape, like babies' sleeping suits. A light came on in one of the rooms. The washing blazed into life in front of me and I screamed. Then my brother screamed. We both noticed at the same time that the washing hanging out to dry was rabbits, still with their heads and ears on. Rabbit skins, black, white, spotted, small, large. Their dried-up legs were bumping painfully against our faces. There was one rabbit hanging there that looked as if someone had outlined its eyes in black kohl. We used to call her Cleopatra. We took to our heels. There were so many of them. The smell was suffocating. We used to hug them, bury our faces in their fur and give them rides in my brother's car, and now we were running away from them. They followed us with their dead, carrot-colored eyes. Their perpetual movement, their different colors had staved off the monotony of the desert for us, and yet now we could have been escaping from a forest fire. We flew along the asphalt road shrieking. When the houses and gardens of the compound came in sight we cried louder, hoping that somebody would come out to ask what was wrong, so that we could describe the horrors we had seen. But music, the smell of food, the murmuring of voices was all that came out of these peaceful houses.

"Why did he do it?" asked my brother. Then, as if he

had worked out the answer for himself, he clutched my hand tighter and said, "He killed them like he wanted to kill me. Why?"

"We'll kill him," I said.

"We'll hit him," replied my brother.

"No. We'll kill him. I'll slit his throat," I said breathlessly, running as if Bus were getting away from me.

"No. No. We'll just hit him," said my little brother. Covering his eyes, he shouted tearfully, "No! We're not going to slit his throat."

Perhaps we would give him some of the sleeping tablets my mother sometimes took, or slip poison into his food. Where would we get poison from? My father would sack him as soon as he found out. But that was too good for him. He'd find another job. We had to take revenge. I was so full of rage and fear that I didn't think about whether I would be punished for disobeying orders and going to the servants' quarters.

My entrance did not have the impact on my mother that I had anticipated. Her eyes remained fastened on the book in front of her. She only looked up curiously when she heard the words "servants' quarters" and then suddenly seemed to take notice of our tears. She jumped up to see what was wrong, and when she made out what we were saying she burst out laughing, asking us to repeat our tale and dissolving into helpless laughter again. She called Bus and when he didn't answer, she carried on as if she were talking to herself, saying she had never pictured him as being so sharp. His only job before he came to the desert and worked in people's houses had been carrying messages between villages in his own country, and now here he was getting the compound's children to raise rabbits and selling their meat and fur: a profitable operation with very low costs.

She called him again. I knew he'd gone to fetch water from the tank as his bike and the plastic water container weren't by the door. I let her call, still shocked by her amused reaction. I grabbed hold of my little brother's hand violently, to show her how angry I was. How could she talk to us like this when we were hysterical? I wanted to tell her how unfeeling she was, how all grown-ups were unbelievably stupid and cruel, and I didn't want to grow up. I left the room in a fury, as I had entered it.

I picked up my brother and carried him to bed. We hadn't had anything to eat or drink, because we didn't want to go into the kitchen and see the murderer. We didn't change into our nightclothes or brush our teeth. I held my brother tight, wiping away his tears and promising him that we would take revenge. We fell asleep with the salty taste of our tears still in our mouths.

We woke up the next morning to find a little white rabbit at the breakfast table, looking at us helplessly.

Instead of putting out his hand to touch it, my brother looked at me, waiting to see my reaction. I rushed impulsively to pick it up and felt it trembling as I held it to my face and kissed it. Then I gave it to him and he took hold of it hesitantly. Bus came up, peeling a potato, and asked him for a thank-you kiss, but my brother ran over to me and we rushed out of the kitchen together.

I Sweep the Sun off Rooftops

Like a thirsty horse I made for the water. But I wasn't thirsty. I was on fire. I threw the water over the English boy and his friend, and fire blazed in my head and heart and between my legs.

Images kept on coming at me that, like an enraged horse, I tried to resist, defiantly tossing my head high, but each new picture flashing into my mind provoked me more and I shook my head frantically from side to side.

Seeing Saad laid out on the floor, dumb and silent;

Saad, whose mighty voice had welled up from his entrails. Now his wife seemed to have snatched his voice to lament for him, joined by her daughters, by his aunts and sisters, all beating their faces and rubbing ash and black soot onto their cheeks.

The English pigeon devouring the remains of the couscous without a pause, immersing its whole beak and head in the grains while I smiled at it, saying, "You seem to like couscous from a packet. I suppose it's because you're an English pigeon. You're used to things out of packets."

Aisha's insistent words in the grain store, as she shook her gold earrings and the bangles on her wrist, urging me to stay at home, but I could only gaze at her shoes and marvel at how exactly they matched her handbag.

Then I am standing in Aisha's house with its Moroccan furniture and Moroccan smell, hardly able to believe that I'm in London.

The letter with my name in English on the envelope, a Moroccan stamp, and a list of requests from my family for a white bridal veil for my sister, surgical stockings for my brother and a china dish for my mother.

Offering the blond English boy—the one I was throwing water at now—half my lunch, and sitting there full of gratitude because he smiled, because he liked the taste of the piece of chicken dipped in cumin and saffron and he was smiling at me for the first time. I wanted his approval because he was English. I wanted the approval of everyone from the bus conductor to the Pakistani shopkeeper, because he owned a shop and spoke English. Being lost in the Underground, tears running down my cheeks. Learning to decipher the names of the stations. Learning the letters by heart as if they were magic signs.

I was throwing water at the English boy and his friend and they were yelling, "She's crazy. Jesus Christ, she's completely crazy."

He started up at my scream and I saw the purple blood on him and on me. Then he jumped to his feet as if he'd been bitten by a snake, shouting, "You're a virgin! You're still a virgin! I don't understand you."

I didn't chew my fingers with regret at giving him my virginity, furious at my weakness in lying down for him, and taking this boy in my arms just because he was English, a citizen of that great nation which had once ruled half the globe; nor did I blame myself for having clung to the notion that I had severed all links with my country just because I had traveled to London alone without any member of my family. Instead of striking my face and grieving aloud because my hymen was no longer intact, I wondered, Is it because he's an Englishman that he doesn't feel proud he's taken my virginity, or is he frightened that now I'll try to force him to marry me?

I tried to tell him that I didn't blame him for deflowering me but he wasn't listening. He just went on saying in a shocked way, as if he had lost his mind, "You're twenty-five, thirty years old? And you're still a virgin? Jesus Christ, I don't understand you. I just don't understand at all."

He didn't go to the bathroom to wash, he stayed in the room. Out of the corner of my eye I watched him wipe himself with Kleenex tissues and drop them on the floor, indifferent to the smears of blood on them. He pulled on his trousers and went quickly over to turn up the music, moving his head from side to side with the beat, then lay facedown on the floor.

I saw myself on the roof of our house as I spread the couscous out to dry on a sheet in the sun for the last time before my journey to London; I could see the whole town in my mind: the tops of the trees, the minaret, the ancient wall that ran round the town. I could think of nothing except going to London and finding my way among its tall buildings sparkling with lights.

I saw the friend of Aisha's helping me escape from her house in London, carrying one of Aisha's children, while I took my suitcase and dragged the other child along with me. I could see Aisha's English neighbor shutting her front door in our faces, and yet all the same we left the two children on the doorstep and ran after I'd pinched their cheeks to make them cry so that she'd have to come out to them.

I walked in the cold London without stockings, without an overcoat, without a sweater. In Marks & Spencer there were hundreds of dresses and sweaters and beautiful night-dresses. I paid the woman at the cash register and smiled at her. She smiled back and said the coat I'd chosen was really pretty. I was overjoyed. She approved of my taste and I'd given her the right amount of money for the red coat, which I still haven't worn.

I bent eagerly over the vacuum cleaner, as if it were a magic broom to transport me to another world, from poverty to riches. The implements available for cleaning here were as many and varied in color and smell as the places I had to clean. Aisha's gold chain, which I had hidden among my clothes, was in my hands one moment and the next on the counter in the Oxford Street goldsmith's.

The red of my anger bubbled up like the rosy orange juice squeezed by the machines in the tourist street in our town. It ran down between my eyes and made me see everything blood-red, even though seconds before my mind had conjured up a pleasing vision: the English boy's sister. She was polite, she gave me a small box of chocolates with a thank-you card and kissed me and shook my hand when she came for Sunday dinner. She had been different from her brother and from his friends, who used to visit us and make themselves at home in my clean room and on the clean bed, delighted to find a video and a cassette recorder, who ate my nice food and listened to loud music and swallowed the drink they brought with them. They all said they wanted to visit my country and I nodded my head, promising it wouldn't cost them a penny, thinking how the people in the town would crowd around them, look at their colored hair, some of it short and some long. I smiled at them, heaped more food onto their plates, poured more mint tea or coffee into their cups. I wanted their approval, even if they did smell so terrible, the reek of their hair in its stiff, bright tufts mixing with the fumes of alcohol.

I began to alter my standards of hospitality, offering them my pale, cold face when their music grew louder, when they began laughing among themselves and didn't take the trouble to explain their jokes to me as they had before, or repeat their words until I understood what they were saying. The English boy showed the others all the implements and products I had collected for cleaning and disinfecting, telling them I had a mania for cleanliness, and I'd once decided to wash all his clothes and he'd had to stay indoors the whole day.

I felt revolted by them and began to sleep in the hall, dragging a pillow and a wool blanket off the bed and leaving the room to them, in the hope that they would understand my anger, that they would no longer stay till the early hours of the morning, stepping over me as I lay asleep, leaving overflowing ashtrays and empty glasses and cans and bottles strewn about the floor. Sometimes they were so drunk they fell asleep where they were and lay without pillows or covers until I returned from work, and then I would rage at them in Arabic, telling them that thanks to them my room was no better than the Italian's pig farm on the outskirts of our town; we used to spit on the ground whenever we went near it, shouting exclamations of disgust, even though all we could see of it was the outer fence.

Why was I doing this? Pouring water over them while they yelled at each other? Perhaps similar things happened in the neighboring rooms, which were occupied by all different people. Their noise had stopped me from sleeping: shouting, shattering glass, the word *police* echoing here and there.

How glad I'd been in those first nights with him. I'd believed he would protect me from these sounds. Now they were happening right inside my own room. I tried to shout like the two of them, but my cry came out strangled and distorted; I still didn't know how to express my anger in English. So I reverted to the role of crazy horse, raging bull: wheeling, rearing, plunging, now attacking, now drawing back. Were they shouting? No, they were laughing. Actually laughing.

It was the music that brought me in from the hall where I had been lying. A single note repeated over and over again, throbbing in my head, making my chest tighten. I had to be rid of them, I decided. I had to be rid of the English boy. I'd give him a choice: he could either stay on his own or leave. I knew he had no home, but that wasn't my problem. I was going to pull the tape out of the machine, interrupt the music right in the middle of the song. It had been on loud all evening, and now it was the early hours of the morning. They had no sensitivity, no conscience.

I charged like a bull. When I saw no one in the middle of the room, which had been full of music and smoke and pungent with the smell of hashish, I thought he must have forgotten to turn off the music before he went to sleep. I found myself thinking affectionately that I ought to be straightforward with him; the English liked that. Perhaps he didn't understand why I'd become so angry and distant. Suddenly I stopped and stood still, staring in amazement. A man was lying by his side. They were both naked. They were lying in each other's arms. I saw their uncircumcised members as clear as day and shuddered. That was the first time I'd seen a man's penis up close and my mouth and throat went dry. I went dry between my legs for several seconds, then I charged again. Shocked, they started up, but they made no attempt to cover their nakedness.

Then, as if they'd recovered from the surprise, they began to laugh, snorting and giggling in delight at the water being thrown at them, like two children playing a game.

I must be dreaming, seeing the opposite of what I thought I was seeing. In reality they should have been dumbfounded, wishing the floor would open up and swallow them in their embarrassment. Or hiding themselves from me, thinking up a whole range of lies and excuses. How would the English boy go on living now that he'd been found out?

They continued to call on Jesus Christ, trying to dry themselves off, then laughing again. The English boy pointed to my face, unable to control his mirth. I must have looked like the mad ape that wandered the streets of our town with its gypsy owner.

Their laughter so infuriated me that I began to have thoughts of revenge. But how, when he had nothing that I could take by force, steal, hide, break in front of him, tear up or trample underfoot, to vent my rage and spite? All he owned were the clothes on his back and a few cassettes, which I'd partly paid for anyway. I looked wildly about me a hundred times, unable to think what to do; then I threw my coat on over my nightdress, pulled woolen socks over the wool trousers I wore to protect me from the cold, and ran to the door, without listening to what his friend was trying to say to me. I went out and slammed the door behind me, turning the key in the lock as if I wanted to safeguard the proof of the crime and its only witnesses, repeating the same English phrase over and over again: "Just you wait and see." Then I went on in Arabic: "You'll be sorry. Everybody's going to know. I should have noticed. You were with me for a whole week and you might just as well have been a girl, or a boy without balls. What was I doing admiring you for being so well behaved, sitting there for hours content to have your arm around me? I even said to myself, 'He's English and he understands.' Still, I wanted you to go all the way with me, and London's far away. I'll never go back home. I'll always live here now. I should have guessed. How was I to know? If you'd had a big fat bottom I might have guessed. But you're all scrawny. Your bum's hardly bigger than a fist. I'm crazy. I let your white flesh and your skinny body and your blond hair blot out things that would have made me shudder at home."

I rang his sister from a pay phone. When she heard my voice, she asked dryly, "What do you want?"

"Your brother—" I began.

She cut in. "Are you getting me out of bed at this hour to talk to me about my brother?" she demanded.

"It's urgent," I replied.

At this she changed her tone, and asked quickly, "Is he all right?"

I told her what I had found out. She shouted at me, accusing me of being crazy to wake her up for that and telling me to keep my nose out of her brother's business, especially since it was nothing to do with me. As her parting shot she told me never to phone her at this time of the night again, but then her anger seemed to have woken her and she continued, "I know you went to a lot of trouble over the meal, but my brother's sexual proclivities aren't any of your business, or mine either."

"Bitch," I screamed down the phone at her, then, remembering how much they liked dogs here, I shouted in English, "Whore! Whore!"

I walked along, trembling with anger and misery, not through the London of beautiful houses and clean streets that I'd dreamed of, where people wore only elegant, expensive clothes, nor between buildings glittering with lights that soared into the clouds, but in the darkness among the shadows of trees planted at infrequent intervals and council houses with their unlit windows, all alike; I passed people asleep, protected from the cold in cardboard boxes, and rubbish in untidy heaps or neatly tied up in black plastic bags, and empty milk bottles with traces of sour milk lingering in them.

A voice rose from a heap of clothes on the pavement, accompanied by the stench of alcohol-laden breath, a voice begging for a drink or money to buy a drink. I used to smile at people who stopped me in the street, not knowing what they wanted at first, until I discovered that there were actually beggars in London. I gave them money, full of pride that I was richer than at least one English person, even if he was a beggar.

I walked along with something boring a hole between my legs. Now I was conscious of Aisha's words when we stood together in the storeroom and she tried to dissuade me from going to London: "Go alone to London without an aunt or a husband or your mother and they'll say you've sold your soul. You'll be known as a bad girl even if you're as pure as the Prophet's daughter."

Aisha's annual visits home had sown the seed of travel in my spirit and this seed had grown and opened out and reached my eyes and tongue. On her last visit I'd been unable to take my eyes off her gold earrings and her bangles. I'd dragged her into the storeroom and begged her to take me to London, saying my family wouldn't allow me to go without her. It was not only her matching handbag and high-heeled shoes that fired my enthusiasm. The smell of couscous and other grains that filled the air constantly reminded me of my own situation. All I wanted to smell from now on was the fragrance of England, which Aisha exuded. I urged her to listen to me and to feel what I was feeling. Then I took off my little gold earrings and felt in the folds of my dress for all the money I'd saved or stolen over the years, and placed both the money and the earrings in the palm of her hand, forcing her fingers shut around them. As

I gave her an exaggerated account of my clashes with different members of my family, she continued to discourage me, saying that the work in London was hard and that exile was no easy way of life. I thought she must not like the idea of my going on the plane with her, then coming home every year laden with presents. How could she compare the task of dusting and polishing the magnificent English furniture with the drudgery of cleaning our house, where there were only torn rags, a broom and a pail of water, and you had to go down on your knees to scrub the floor and do the endless piles of washing by hand?

The man at the British customs was much sterner than the magistrate who came from the capital to investigate crimes committed in our town. This man would forget the purpose of his visit, at least for a brief spell, and the fact that he was on official business, and drink tea and eat a good meal in the prosecutor's house, crack jokes and make amiable conversation, and sleep through the heat of the day. The British official behind his high desk asked me numerous questions, which I didn't understand. When all I could reply were the two forlorn words, "No English," he asked me if I knew French. I nodded my head to find I had opened Ali Baba's cave merely by answering all his questions with the one French word *oui.* His features relaxed and he stamped my passport. Without realizing it, he had let me know that using French words, however few and halting, has a bewitching effect upon everything in London, animate and inanimate alike.

I'd woken up the next morning at Aisha's place, not convinced that I was really in London: her flat was like any flat at home with the same smell, the same colored ottomans and rugs, the same pictures on the walls, the brass tray in the middle of the room, and the loud shrieks and wails of her two children puncturing the air. However, this sensation evaporated as soon as I looked out the window, when I realized how imprisoned I was by my ignorance, which Aisha seized upon, exploiting the fact that I didn't know how to flush the toilet, work the shower, turn on the oven or boil the electric kettle to make tea, and that I couldn't understand what her older child or her next-door neighbor said. I couldn't even answer the phone. Inventing far-fetched excuses, she left me trapped in her flat and made no attempt to help me look for work.

From the window I saw the flats opposite, their even lines making them look like children's drawings. Noisy voices floated through their windows. I let my gaze wander to the open grassy strip at the side of the block, which was almost completely empty of life, and then onto the red buses and cars hurrying along the main road. Fixing my eyes on them, I couldn't help cursing Aisha, wishing she were dead, swearing by the Prophet Muhammad that I would have my revenge because it was she who was stopping me from walking those streets and riding in those red buses to find work and a home of my own. When Aisha returned from work, coming through the door weighed down with plastic shopping bags, her coat smelling of perfume mixed with cigarette smoke, I gave a shiver of anger: I wanted to carry shopping bags like that and wear a coat like hers!

Since everything seemed out of my reach I was reduced to making friends with the pigeons, who were everywhere, and whose gentle murmurings I'd grown accustomed to hearing. I put the remains of our dinner on the window ledge to attract them, and when one of them alighted near me I called to it, "Taste this couscous, steamed and mixed with oil, English pigeon, and tell me if it's nice."

I'd been amazed that in London you could buy ready-made couscous in packets, and that the English used it in their cooking. I'd imagined that they would eat food fit for kings, and look upon our food with distaste.

I left Aisha's prison in the following way: one day a woman from the same town as Aisha and me came to pick up her sewing machine. She asked me if I was happy here and I sighed. She responded with an even deeper sigh. I found myself lying to her, although my lies seemed to me to represent the truth as soon as I was out of Aisha's house. I told her how Aisha kept a close watch on what I ate and drank, and how I had to take care of the house and children to pay for my board and lodging. The woman nodded her head in agreement and remarked, "Yes. Everybody says Aisha's become like an Englishwoman. She must have saved herself more than fifty pounds a week having you here, because she used to pay her neighbor to look after the two children for her while she was out at work."

Immediately we joined forces against Aisha, criticizing her and insulting her. The visitor told me things about her that I didn't believe, but still I nodded my head as if to confirm what she said. For my part, I told her that I was sure Aisha had a lover and we began searching for proof. We broke into the single, locked cupboard, and although we only found some new clothes and shoes with jewelry stuffed up inside the toes, we assured each other that Aisha received money from her lover and liked leaving me in the house with the children because it made it easier to cheat on her husband.

Only the walls heard this delirious talk, but I was suddenly seized by a guilty fear, and became convinced that the two children were taking it in and that it was ringing in Aisha's ears at work, and I rushed to pack my suitcase before she came back. The visitor left, forgetting to take her sewing machine, and I left with her, convinced that I would never see Aisha again and that news of my forcing the lock on her cupboard would reach my hometown well amplified, so that I'd end up accused of stealing all of Aisha's possessions.

I took the woman's advice and looked for work that paid by the hour. I discovered that time was money and threw myself into cleaning offices, restaurants and hospitals. Picturing the pounds mounting up in my handbag, I pushed myself harder, indifferent to the veins aching with fatigue and the bits of my body that cried out with exhaustion and craved sleep. I only stopped working frenziedly hour after hour when I met the English boy I'd just thrown water over moments before.

I left the woman's house as soon as I found work and a room to rent. When I was told that I'd have to share a kitchen and bathroom with strangers, I couldn't help thinking how this would astound the people at home, how they would snort with laughter at the idea that this could really happen in England, mother of civilization. The English boy used to work in the hospital for a day at a time, and then be off for several days. At tea breaks and lunchtime I never saw him eat more than a bar of chocolate or a biscuit. I never saw him talk to anybody. He would just put his headphones on and close his eyes. He had blond hair, light eyes and a thin face. I suppose I fancied him although I told myself that it was just that I felt sorry for him. I decided to offer him some food. When I approached and held a piece of chicken out to him he opened his eyes and at first refused to take it. I insisted and he put out his hand, asking me if I was sure. I smiled. I no longer took what the English said seriously. "Are you sure?" they ask without fail, regardless of whether you are offering them a cup of tea or paying their bus fare.

After eating the piece of chicken dipped in cumin and saffron, which he seemed to have liked, he asked me where I came from. I told him and it was as if I'd opened Heaven's door. His face softened, his pupils grew bigger, and his irises went deep green like olive oil. Enthusiastically he told me that he'd always wanted to visit Morocco, live there even, and that our hashish was the best of all. Was it true, he inquired anxiously, was it really cheap there? I answered him with lies, happy that he was so interested after I'd been certain that he'd never say a word to me: I told him that I grew it myself, my family grew it, and it was everywhere, like green grass and empty milk bottles in London; it was really amazing hashish: wherever I threw its seeds it sprang up like flames leaping into the air.

Dreaming of the hashish and the sunshine he said, "You left all that sun for the sake of these gray clouds and this miserable country?"

"What can I do with the sun?" I answered. "Sweep it off the rooftops?"

In my imagination I could feel the monotony of the days in my country, the poverty and the nothingness. I remembered the threatening looks of the men in the family, the attentive stares from the ones in the street, my mother's harsh way of talking, and I repeated it to myself. "What can I do with the sun? Sweep it off the roof?"

I was happy in London, free, mistress of my self and my pocket. Here it was impossible not to be happy. At home I thought I was ugly. I listened to the English boy singing the praises of my dark coloring and frizzy hair, felt him kiss me on the cheek with obvious pleasure whenever I cooked a meal and when I came in from work, or when we sat watching television together, and found him waiting for me at the end of the road when for some reason I was late getting back.

I encouraged him to move in one evening after he had taken me to a pub, and I felt this urge to have a hold on all the different sides there were to London. Even though I didn't say a word in the uproar and drank only water, I was standing there like them in the crowds and smoke, proud and glad and sure of myself.

As soon as he entered my room that night, he declared provocatively that I must be rich to have such a bed and quilt, as well as cassettes and a television and a video. He'd expected it, he added, since he noticed that I had my own plate and cup at work, and bought tea for whoever was sitting with me. I smiled, nodding my head, not unhappy if he'd jumped to the wrong conclusions, but surprised that he didn't know the secret of paying by installments. He flung himself down on my bed, trying it out in different positions.

"How clean it is!" he exclaimed. "How comfortable! I've never slept in a bed like this before."

Was I hearing him right or had I missed the point as so often happened? When we talked it was like two people playing ball: sometimes it went into the goal, sometimes it grazed the post, but most of the time it went high in the air and missed completely. He hadn't slept in a bed like that before, yet there were all those advertisements for them on television, and they were on display in shop windows and in most of the big stores in London so that I'd imagined them in all the houses I could see from the bus.

Quite at home in my bed, he fell fast asleep until dawn.

In the little streets and neighborhoods where I wandered, London did not sleep. And when it did, the billboards stayed wide awake. Billboards about films, pop concerts, milk, drugs and AIDS . . . AIDS? My mind suddenly became alert: he was going to die of AIDS. I should tell him, extending my finger in a threatening manner: You'll die of AIDS. Then I found myself shouting, inside my head, *I'll die of AIDS. Oh my God!*

Then partly reassured, I thought, He entered me twice, but he came outside me. Then again I cried out in terror, wordlessly, Who knows? Maybe a germ slipped out of his prick and landed on me. And with an involuntary movement I raised my eyes to the sky—where God was—beseeching Him, wanting Him to see my fear and my contrition. But I couldn't see the moon or the stars, only the gloomy sky. I lowered my head quickly, as if to acknowledge the truth spoken by the old woman Khadija when she heard of my decision to travel to London. "Foreigners have no God," she claimed, as if she wanted to weaken my resolve and then, correcting herself and asking God's pardon, she changed this to "Our God, the God of Islam, is different from theirs in the West."

Then, again asking God's forgiveness, she said that there was no god but God, and the trouble was that Westerners didn't follow His instructions or live by His law. At this she rose, washed her mouth ten times to make amends and performed twenty prostrations for her scepticism.

I had to go back to the room, especially now that there was someone following me. As I accelerated my pace I asked myself what I was doing here, and I didn't know the answer. Why didn't I go home to my own country, taking with me the sheet that bore the stains of my virginity? I had purposely left it unwashed, stuffing it in a suitcase because I might need to spread it out on my bridegroom's bed in the dark of the night. Bridegroom? I would save some money and then I would find a man to marry me, especially if I promised to bring him to London. But why was I here? Was it because I was out of reach of the prying eyes of the people in my town, the constant questions from the men in my family about my comings and goings, and my mother's interrogations about why I slept on my stomach, or why I took so long in the bathroom? The God of my far-off country must bear that in mind, and still love me. Now I had to be on my guard against AIDS and the Devil. I opened the front door and heard the voice of Warda Al-Jazairiyya flooding through the door of my room. Pushing it open, I was confronted by a tall, blond, green-eyed version of myself, the Englishman's friend dressed up in my clothes, with my kohl on his eyes, wearing a pair of my earrings. He was swaying his head in time to the Arab song.

I stood before my blond other self. Now the haze lifted and all the images became clear. I no longer had to push away the picture of Saad laid out on the floor, or banish from my imagination the sound of his huge voice, louder than the roaring of the wind, dumb forever. The women of the family struck their faces and smeared them with soot. Saad had taken his own life the night the news had gone around that he'd been caught sleeping with a traveling shepherd. He could no longer speak: he had swallowed his voice, choking on the words, while his wife's voice, which had always been quiet and low before, rose high into the air, followed by those of his daughters and his sisters. When Saad's note proclaiming his innocence was discovered there was an outcry in the town. Saad's family rushed to try and have their revenge on the witness who had announced the news like someone possessed, and who now cared less about Saad's death than about convincing the whole community of what he had seen in the hut that burning noonday. The town was divided between those who wanted Saad's name cleared and those who wanted the accusation against him proven even after his death. His soul would have no repose and would hover over the place, flying through the night.

As I remembered, I laughed. My blond self laughed at the people of my town. I imagined Saad lying down with the English boy and the two of them flirting and giggling together. The boy came over and put his arm around me, as if he could not quite believe my laughter and my lack of agitation. I smiled at both of them and told his friend my clothes suited him. He asked if I had a caftan he could borrow. I shook my head regretfully—I hadn't brought it with me, thinking the English would look down on my caftan with its silver belt—although I saw garments like it selling here at huge prices. I was still laughing. I imagined the beggar from the London streets sitting with the old woman Khadija in my town; the conductor on the red London bus talking to Hammouda the postman; the English boy's friends playing with Khadija's grandson, especially Margaret, whose hair reminded me of the colored duster Khadija's grandson had pleaded for every time he saw it in the market, thinking it was a toy or a bird. I saw Margaret talking to Saniyya in the bathhouse. I saw people springing up from the ground or coming down out of the sky, boarding red buses, jabbering in English. Englishmen climbing the ancient wall with their bowler hats and black umbrellas and Englishwomen pushing their strollers along the winding muddy roads.

The television blared, and my attention was caught by the electricity advertisements: an electric stove, an electric heater, an electric boiler. I'd have to buy an electric boiler to replace the gas one, which had been leaking for a week now. The gas man had told us not to use it or else it would blow up, and had stuck on a red warning sign to remind us.

I turned, intending to ask the English boy why he lived with me, why he liked my company. Once he had said I showed him a concern that he had never met with before, even from his parents, and that he would love to visit my country one day. At the time I didn't believe him because I wasn't used to hearing the truth from people's lips, preferring to believe what I thought rather than what I heard.

Instead I found myself thinking, AIDS. I looked at the two of them: "You ought to go and have a blood test."

I was thinking I would boil the sheets that evening and ask the chemist for a powerful disinfectant and give myself a vinegar douche to get rid of all the germs inside me.

They went into the kitchen and I started to tidy the room, gathering the plates from here and there and scattering the remains of the food on the window ledge. The pigeons flocked around it immediately, though dawn was only just breaking. I knew the neighbors complained that this habit of mine encouraged the pigeons to come up to the windows, but I didn't care. "Eat up," I told the nearest bird. "You're lucky I'm feeding you, not eating you. Where I come from, if we see a pigeon we throw a stone at it. If it falls we accept our good fortune, kill it and eat it. If it carries on flying we shrug our shoulders and say, It's the angels' turn today. You're not beautiful, you're not white, or even a nice light brown. You're gray and black like a big rat, but I love you because you're English and you wait for me every day."

The Funfair

My fiancé, Farid, insisted that I should go with him and his family to visit his grandmother's grave on the eve of the feast. I had always thought this custom was for old or lonely people, who took comfort from sitting with their dead relatives. They say there's nothing like visiting a cemetery for curing depression. I had not been aware of my own parents visiting family graves on special days, although once when I was little I prayed fervently that somebody I didn't know in the family would die so that I could go inside one of the buildings people put up around their graves. I had gone with our cook to her house overlooking the cemetery—an occasion that must have remained imprinted on my mind—and from then on I'd pictured the dead people living in those burial chambers, like us in our houses, only different: perhaps they moved about without making any sound, or stayed in bed all the time.

In those days the tombs seemed strange to me, with their engraved cupolas, the color of sand. They stood among a few faded trees and mounds of sandy earth that were perfect for rolling down. When I heard dogs barking and cats yowling, I was sure they were the guardians of these tombs.

We called in at Farid's parents' house. As I made to reply to his father's greeting, his mother appeared from nowhere and asked me disapprovingly why I wasn't wearing the diamond earrings.

"Diamonds for the cemetery?" I asked.

"Why not?" She nodded. "Everyone's going to be there, I know, and they'll say he only gave you a ring when you were engaged."

Then she vanished and returned with a brooch of precious stones and came toward me to pin it on my dress. I took a step backward, insisting as diplomatically as I could that I didn't like brooches. Turning again toward her room she replied impatiently, "All right. Wear my marcasite earrings. But everybody will recognize them."

I looked beseechingly at Farid and he said to her, "I don't want her to wear any jewelry."

Only then did she notice the bunch of white roses I was holding. She took them from me, smelling them and calling on the Prophet in her delight, then rushed to put them in a vase with some other flowers. The price of them had made me hesitate, but they had looked as if they were just waiting for someone to appreciate their fragrant beauty. I justified buying them on the grounds that they weren't for me, and that anyway, from now on there was no need for me to feel a pang of conscience every time I bought something expensive, since I was going to marry a wealthy man. Farid told his mother that the flowers were for the grave. "What a shame. They're lovely," she replied, continuing to arrange them in the vase.

Farid signaled to me, and I understood that I shouldn't pursue the subject of the flowers. I looked about me in an attempt to escape from my embarrassment at her behavior and pretended to be interested in the content of the baskets by the door: pastries for the feast day, bread in unusual shapes and old clothes and shoes.

I sat next to my fiancé in the front of the car, with his mother and father and adolescent sister in the back. The eve of the feast was like the feast itself, the crowded streets throbbing with noise and excitement, and everywhere the sounds of fireworks exploding. I remembered how as children we would rush to examine the peach-colored sand in our socks and shoes as soon as we reached home. Every year when the feast came around, it felt as if we were celebrating it for the first time. My mother would prepare the tray of *kunafa* and we would take it to the communal oven. Although we stood there for ages, our eyes fixed on the baker so that he would remember the tray; he always took it out late and the pastries would be rock hard. All the same we ate them with noisy relish. I remembered the handbag I had especially for the feast, the socks I wore even at the height of summer, the shiny shoes, the hair ribbons. We used to visit all our relatives, including those who lived at a distance and were hardly related to us at all. We would knock on their doors and wish them well, not meaning what we said. We knew the uncle who said he had no change on him was lying and would sit for ages on his doorstep before we rushed off to the swings and the pickle sellers, discussing the rumor that the feast was going to last a day or two longer this year for the children's benefit.

People spent the whole of this feast-day eve in the cemetery. The children wore their brightest clothes. Amplified voices recited the Quran, and at the same time popular songs blared out from radios and cassette recorders. There were women selling dates and palm leaves. One was smoking and the others shared a joke, their tattooed chins quivering with laughter. Fool beans and falafel, fruit juice and pickles of many varieties and colors were all on sale at the entrance to the cemetery. I thought I would have a display of pickles in jars like that in my own house.

Farid's mother stopped at the first vendor she came to, a woman without a tooth in her head, and chose a large quantity of oranges, tangerines and palm leaves. She haggled with her for some time, then gave her a sum of money and walked off. "Lady! Lady!" the woman called after her. When she tried to ease herself up off the ground, I begged Farid to pay her what she was asking: "Poor thing, it's a shame on a day like this."

We hurried to catch up with Farid's mother, elegant in spite of her plumpness, springing over the mud and earth and gravel like a gazelle. She carried her purchases, leaving the baskets to Farid, his father, and his sister, who looked increasingly morose. I found myself walking along beside her. She glanced at her watch and asked if I thought the sun would come out later, then lowering her voice she explained, "I want to go to the club. Have a swim and lie in the sun."

I smiled at her. The noise was deafening. There was the clatter of saucepans and the roar of Primus stoves where the women had spread themselves out to cook in the narrow alleyways and the open spaces between the tombs. The shrieks of children mingled with the voices of the Quran reciters, who moved from grave to grave and in and out of the tombs with burial chambers, which belonged to the comfortably off families. In vain they tried to raise their voices, and their audience—families wanting private recitations for their dead—had to give them all their attention to catch what they were saying, as most of the working reciters were elderly, despite the fact that there were young ones about, leaning against tombstones looking bored. I watched Farid's mother darting from one to another, and all of them promising to find their way to her sooner or later with the help of the cemetery caretaker. When one of the younger ones approached her offering his services, she pretended not to notice him. Angrily Farid asked her why she had snubbed him and she answered, "Old men have more merit in the eyes of the Lord."

Perhaps this was because the young faces didn't bear the marks of grief and suffering like the old ones.

We went into a courtyard with a little garden around it where there were graves with pink and white ornamental headstones. Farid said they belonged to his great-grandfather and two great-uncles, who had asked to be buried in the garden, which looked green and moist as if someone had recently watered it. Then we crossed the courtyard into the main family tomb and found it crammed with members of the family, a Quran reciter and dishes of dates and cucumbers and tangerines. The grave itself was festooned with palm leaves. Why are we sitting in here, right next to the grave? I wondered.

I saw disappointment, then anger on the face of my fiancé's mother, which she was unable to conceal. "You must have spent the night here" was her first comment to the assembled company. Nobody answered her, but to my amazement they stood up and greeted us, disregarding the recitation of the Quran: Farid's three paternal aunts, his grandfather, the husbands of two of the aunts and their children. They made room for us on wooden chairs, disfigured by time and neglect, and we all sat down except for Farid's mother, who began spreading more palm leaves over the grave until it had almost vanished from sight. Then she took out pastries, bread, dates, cucumbers, tangerines and glasses for tea. She put some pastries and dates in a bag and went up to the Quran reciter, thrusting it into his hands. He stopped in the middle of his recitation to mumble his thanks and handed the bag to a boy who was sitting at his feet counting out notes and coins before putting them in his pocket.

Farid's mother asked him all of a sudden how much he took from each family. "Depends how much time they want," the boy answered slyly.

"How much?" she insisted. "Last year, for example."

"Last year was last year," he replied. Then, peering into the bag, he named an amount that made Farid's mother gasp. "That's the same as a checkup at the doctor's," she remarked. I met my fiancé's eyes and we almost laughed aloud.

There was uproar outside, then the caretaker appeared, accompanied by a sheikh. When they heard the recitation in progress, the sheikh tried to retreat, but Farid's mother grabbed his hand and pulled him in. In spite of the family's obvious disapproval she led him over to where her daughter was sitting, while he murmured, "I mustn't poach from someone else."

Impatiently she answered him, "Just relax. He'll get his share and you'll get yours."

The sheikh obeyed and sat listening to his colleague, nodding his head with feeling, while the aunts' faces registered annoyance; one of them sighed and another turned her face away. Farid's mother declared, "It's not a feast every day, and we want to be sure our dead go to heaven."

Then she approached the caretaker, wishing him well, and counted out some money into his hand, enunciating the amount in an audible voice. "I hope this place isn't opened up again as soon as our backs are turned?" she inquired sharply.

"What do I carry a weapon for?" countered the caretaker.

"No. You know what I mean," she said. "We heard that the previous caretaker used to rent out our tomb as if it was a hotel."

"That's why he's the previous caretaker. You know I don't even let kids come through here."

I thought that relief was at hand when from outside the smell of kebab and meatballs wafted in, making my nostrils twitch. The blind reciter rose to his feet and was led away by the boy, while the newcomer began chanting prayers. I looked around the tomb room, especially at the aunts' faces. They shifted their gaze from me to Farid's mother and sister, and back again. When our eyes met we exchanged smiles, as if they knew what I was thinking and agreed: It doesn't matter that Farid's mother is difficult, and I don't have any sort of relationship with her. Farid's family all love him, even though he does exactly what she says.

The reciter paused to clear his throat and immediately one of the aunts turned to me and said she hadn't expected me to be so pretty, in spite of the descriptions she'd heard, and only an illness had kept her away from my engagement party. Another asked if we'd found an apartment and what area we were thinking of. I answered these questions in all innocence at first, but from their expressions and the way Farid kept trying to catch my eye, I felt I must be on sensitive ground as far as his mother was concerned. Sure enough, she interrupted and said there was no urgency about renting a place, her house had big rooms and was Farid's as much as it was hers.

When I replied to the aunts that we were planning a simple wedding, just the family, Farid's mother announced, as if she hadn't heard a word I'd said, that we'd be holding it in one of the big hotels. When I told them that my wedding dress was secondhand, and had been worn first in the twenties, she was unable to hide her alarm. It was then I realized a state of war existed between Farid's mother and the aunts and regretted ever opening my mouth. From their loaded questions and the way they looked at one another after each of my replies, I could tell that they were using me to attack her in her most vulnerable spot. She protested, almost in a scream, "God forbid! You're wearing a dress that someone else has worn, to your wedding? That's out of the question!"

"Is it white?" inquired one of the aunts, provoking Farid's mother to still greater anguish.

"White, black, what's the difference?" she shouted. "It's out of the question. Marisa has to make it. I promised her. She'll be upset."

"Upset!" remarked one of them, laughing. "She's got more work than she can handle. She'll be delighted."

"I know you're jealous because Marisa's going to make it," screamed back Farid's mother.

For a moment I forgot where I was. The walls were

gray and the visitors' chairs blocked out the tombstone and the palm leaves. We could have been in somebody's sitting-room. Farid's father and the third aunt's husband interrupted the argument, coming to stand behind their wives' chairs. "The clothes. Aren't we going to give them to the caretaker?" asked Farid's father, changing the subject.

"I forgot all about them," she replied. "May death forget me!" Then she whispered something in his ear. When he didn't make any comment, she said, "Who'd like some tea?" She went over into a corner where there was a Primus stove I hadn't noticed before. As she pumped it, she asked, "What do you think about building onto the tomb? Another room, a little kitchen, a bathroom?"

Nobody answered. They were all absorbed in their own private conversations. She repeated, "We need to extend the tomb. Farid's father agrees. What do you say?"

"Extend it!" scoffed one of the aunts. "To hear you talking anyone would think a tomb was just like an apartment!"

"What I meant," Farid's mother corrected herself, "is that we should buy an old, abandoned tomb."

Another aunt seized on her words: "And have our dead mixed up with other people's? That's madness!"

"I mean, we should buy a plot of ground, even if it's a little way off."

The voices rose and fell. Farid's cousins and sister whispered scornfully to one another. Farid brought me a glass of tea. Meanwhile, his mother continued to ask at intervals, "What do you say?"

"What do we say?" answered one of the aunts at last. "Nobody's in a position to lay out money on tombs and suchlike, that's what we say."

Farid's mother drew a triumphant breath: "Farid's got a marvelous job, thank God, and . . ."

I looked with embarrassment at Farid, who was shaking his head like someone who wanted help. He said sheepishly, "Why do you need to mention that?"

His mother must have felt from this response that he was siding with his aunts against her, but she went on. "I mean God's made you rich enough to pay for the new tomb."

She seemed to gain strength from his silence, and had the look of a cat when the mouse is finally cornered. But the spiteful looks of the other women snatched victory from her grasp. "We know your stories," they seemed to say. "You want to tell your friends that you've got a big new tomb. A villa! A three-story villa with marble stairs and wrought-iron gates!"

"Have you ever heard of anyone visiting the family tomb and sitting almost on top of the graves?" shouted Farid's mother. "We must have a separate room to sit in."

"We used to be able to use the one you gave the caretaker," interrupted one of the aunts.

"At least there's only him and his wife," persisted Farid's mother. "Surely that's better than having a family taking it over, with children clambering over our tombstones like apes, and then not being able to get rid of them."

"And what's wrong with being buried in the garden?" continued the aunt in a superior tone. "You don't have to be inside the room."

"Your grandfather liked the idea of being buried in the garden—that's his business," yelled Farid's mother. "I and my family want to be buried inside."

In a whisper, as if divulging a secret, Farid's father said, "Listen to me. Land prices are going to soar. People are going to start living in these buildings on a regular basis. And anyway, what's wrong with our family having the very best?"

"I know," answered his sister. "But is it reasonable to expect you to pay while we stand with our arms folded? You know, the children are at university and there are the monthly payments to keep up with and all our other commitments . . ."

"I'm ready to fall in with anything," said her husband.

His intervention seemed to irritate Farid's mother and she snapped back at him, "In any case, your wife won't be buried here. She'll go with your family."

His wife ignored her and said, "Look. Just look around. This tomb's big. You couldn't call this a small area."

But Farid's mother came back at her with a reply that unnerved me like a physical blow. All along I hadn't believed that the family's scheming and arguing over a peaceful grave in its midst could be serious. I told myself it must be a family joke, and anyway it had nothing to do with me, even Farid's helping to pay.

Standing in the middle of the room, Farid's mother declared, "No. It's not as big as you imagine. There's me, my husband, and now Farid's about to become two, and then there'll be his children."

Her words frightened me. Death wasn't as distant as it had been to me. I didn't think of it, as a child might, as something that wouldn't happen to me. Trying to make a joke, I said, "Should we be planning for our afterlife when we're not yet married?"

"We're saying prices are going to soar," intervened Farid's father, seizing on the same pretext as before.

I knew that all eyes were on me, especially the aunts', begging me to save them from Farid's mother's claws. But I lacked the strength even to save myself and abandoned myself to the terrifying thought that one day I'd be here in this room underneath a tombstone, with one for Farid and each of my children. We'd all end up here and our children's children would sit like us now, sipping tea, arguing, eating dates.

The raised voices of the men, joining in with those of

the women now, brought me back to the present. Farid came to my rescue, taking my hand in his soothingly, and I mumbled, "It's crazy to think about it now."

I don't know how Farid's mother heard what I said; I hardly heard it myself, but she remarked smugly, "Our lives are in God's hands."

This angered me and, unconscious of what I was saying, like a child who wants to contradict for the sake of contradicting, I replied, "I don't want to be buried here."

"You don't have any choice," she said. "When you become part of the family, that's what you have to do. Even your own family wouldn't agree to bury you with them."

I felt as though she were already shoveling earth down on top of me. "No!" I screamed. "No!" I jumped up and rushed to the door. Farid's mother paid no attention even when Farid took hold of me and said reprovingly to her, "Are you happy now?"

"She has to understand, my dear," she said to him, "that whoever lives with us must die with us."

I broke free and ran. He came after me. Outside in the cemetery's main square I caught my breath and leaned against a tombstone while I fastened my sandal. Children were playing with a ball there, disregarding the comments of their mothers and the older women who sat resting from the labors of their cooking. "The dead must be trembling with anxiety down there," remarked one.

I composed myself at last, perhaps at this spectacle of everyday life, or the glimpse of a bird abandoning itself to space, beautiful and oblivious to what was happening below. We stopped beside the car. I knew we would have to wait for his family. I felt I wanted to be free of his hand holding tightly onto mine. I turned my face away, contemplating the washing spread out to dry, the empty bowl resting against one grave, the cooking pot sitting on another, as if it were a table, and the owners of these objects going about their business—victims of the housing crisis, who had squatted in abandoned tombs, rented at the going rate, or simply occupied family tombs prematurely, and adapted them to suit their lives. I saw television and radio aerials in place; and yet Farid's mother wanted a bigger space to house her graves.

When I saw Farid's mother, father and sister appearing in the distance, I felt the breath being knocked out of me. So we were one family, living together, dying together?

Farid's father must have told his wife to keep quiet, as she hadn't uttered a word from the moment she entered the car. His sister tried to make peace with me, and told me about a friend of hers who was a social scientist and was doing a study of the people who lived alongside the dead. She said how the women would be trilling for joy at the birth of a baby, and would fall silent suddenly if they noticed a funeral procession approaching. Their noises of rejoicing would turn to keening, while the men rushed to find which tomb the music was coming from, or the news broadcast, so they could silence it. As soon as the funeral was over, life would return to normal.

But I remained silent. Surrounded by their loud voices, I felt like the ant I'd noticed on the floor of the tomb. It had moved aimlessly along, not knowing that at any moment it could be trodden on and crushed to death. I realized I'd changed my mind about marriage, and I wanted to get out of the car straightaway before I was swallowed up by Farid's mother. I had a vision of the aunts like three witches preparing to serve us all up to the Devil.

I thought I would tell Farid that the reason I'd changed my mind about marrying him wasn't to do with the tomb or where I would be buried. On the contrary, I'd loved all the commotion, and the cemetery itself was like a funfair. Anyway, I didn't like being alone even when I was alive.

Then I decided against this last sentence. I was haunted by the scene of the family in the tomb, and their voices were still ringing in my ears. I resolved to try and like being alone, alive or dead.

The White Peacock of Holland Park

Yasmin stood looking in astonishment at the white peacock. She had not known that nature produced such creatures. Every feather in its long tail had a decorated eye surrounded by a heart, then a bigger heart and finally long eyelashes. The feathers were patterned exactly like blue and green peacock feathers, but they were white. Why had no one thought of white peacock feathers when they wanted to describe the morning mist? She walked up to it, thinking of a way to make it flash its tail. She shouted at it, threw a stone at it—a small one—and barked like a dog. The peacock, its head crowned with white like a fall of fresh snow, continued to move proudly and slowly, drawing its tail behind it, a cloud of fine white lace. She wanted it to come close to her and stand still where she could see it, but it moved on with its haughty, calm gait. Yasmin hurriedly took out a piece of bread that she had brought for her son to feed to the ducks and crumbled it in the peacock's path. It approached, pecked up the crumbs and, failing to find anything else of interest, walked away. God had not forgotten a single ornamentation. She thought, as she followed it, that she would write to her friend in Beirut about it. Then she dismissed the idea guiltily: it would be unthinkable to describe the white peacock to her when she and the others left behind in Beirut were spending their days seeking refuge from the bombardments, trailing between the corridors of their apartment buildings and the underground shelters.

Her son, Ziyad, ran ahead of her, licking an ice cream. She was glad she had gotten him out of Beirut, because for the first time for months he was running about like a child. For two months he had been shut indoors, confined to his room and the kitchen and the passage in between. She looked down at her feet as if she were rediscovering them and began to run delightedly, watching them move. She did not notice that she and Ziyad were alone in the park and the sun had disappeared until the darkness came down suddenly. She caught up with Ziyad and took his hand and hurried to the place where they had come in, but there was a gate barring the way and it was locked. She was both astonished and afraid: it had never occurred to her that parks and gardens had gates which could be locked. Her fear transmitted itself to Ziyad, and he asked anxiously, "Are we going to sleep here?"

"We won't be long. We'll soon be out," she reassured him.

There had to be another gate. All parks had several exits. She walked around and failed to find one: Holland Park seemed to have been transformed into a dense, high forest. The autumn leaves had piled up on the ground and their feet began to sink into them. Although she was afraid, she could not help noticing the beauty of the silent park, visible through the darkness. She stopped, trying to decide which way to go. A few steps, and she was plunging into utter blackness. Sweat trickled from her armpits and her palms felt damp. Her tongue was dry. "Oh God," she said dispiritedly.

She heard Ziyad imitating her: "Oh God."

His voice set up a new current of alarm in her. There must be a telephone. She should make her way back to the first gate. She tried to remember where it was.

It was as if nature knew of her predicament: a man and woman embracing materialized under a tree a few steps away from her. When they became aware of her they walked on. She ran after them, asking them to help her. She and Ziyad and the couple were soon walking together along a path she had not seen before, past a pond where a white goose floated. The man stopped at a wall and jumped over into the street and stood waiting to receive Ziyad. The woman went next and Yasmin found herself scrambling after her, not caring about the height of the wall.

She lay in bed with her eyes closed, remembering being lost in Holland Park, the man and woman embracing under the tree, the dry autumn leaves and the white peacock. She remembered her fear, and to her surprise she liked it. She wanted to be lost again, and to be accompanied by a man. She began to picture it: her heart thumping, her palms sweating, him taking her hand as they wandered around the exits and found them all locked; the two of them in the park, and all the peacocks, in spite of her admiration for them, had flown up into a tree; their long tails, hanging down in a cloud of shimmering whiteness, looked like mist rising from the tree's branches. She longed for this tension, for the decisive moments in a relationship with a man. With her husband, they wouldn't forget the time; her husband would make sure they were out of the park before darkness fell; in fact, she and her husband would never walk in the park together at all.

She switched out the light, closing her eyes and wondering with a smile why the tension in Beirut had not been enough for her. Yet even in the war their tension had been domestic: they thought about food, about water. They did not give vent to their fear by holding each other close or kissing, which was apparently a forbidden activity amid the noise of the explosions, even though it was more real than in peacetime. They needed it to calm them down, to reassure them that love existed despite the violence of war, but instead they began rolling up the rugs with mothballs, having new thick wooden doors made with keys fit for a fortress, and wrapping up the silver in towels rather than themselves in the bedclothes, where they could have gone into their shell and heard nothing but the sound of the waves.

I must find a man to be lost in Holland Park with, so that when darkness falls, and we walk around, our feet sinking into the yellowing leaves, and find all the exits are closed, we are calm and embrace under a tree while we think what to do, then go into the forest and along the narrow path where it is nearly pitch dark.

Yasmin continued to wander around Holland Park, lost in one dense thicket after another, sighing, saying, "Oh God," and never arriving at the perimeter wall. She was always in the middle, caught in the unending maze of paths. In spite of the darkness, she made out the face of a poet whose readings she had attended faithfully before the outbreak of war. He approached her, surprised at this chance meeting, and said that he too was lost. Yasmin led him around the locked exits, along the dark path, and into the forest. He took hold of her hand; she could hear her own breathing and he must have been able to hear it too. Then she stood under a tree, closed her eyes and felt two fiery coals descend on her lips. She trembled. Nobody had kissed her like that before. They walked on and saw the white peacock asleep. To her astonishment the poet squatted down and put out his hand to stroke it; the peacock did not stir. Then he took hold of her hand and passed it over the bird's feathers. The two of them stood up and he held her face and told her that he had noticed her at the poetry evenings: she had been wearing a dress the color of the sea and her face had been sunburned. They did not walk any further, but climbed over the wall and stood on the pavement embracing.

In the morning she could not believe that her meeting with the poet had been a dream. She had dreams regularly, and of men too, but not like this, not with the truthfulness, the reality of this dream. During the day, as she went around London with her son looking for a school for him, admiring the city and feeling pleased to be away from the fear of the war, she was constantly aware of the warmth of the poet's hand, and the feel of his chest as he caught her in his arms when she jumped down off the park wall. She remained uneasy into the afternoon, when she headed for the park and took the same paths she had taken with him. She looked around her: all the little details in the tree trunks and branches, she had seen with him; it even felt the same walking over the piles of dry leaves. The barbed-wire fencing was there, the little pond, the birdsong, the cold sting in the wind. That was the bench where they had sat before the darkness fell. She walked along, wrapping her arms around her chest to protect herself from the cold, while Ziyad crumbled up a piece of bread for the white peacock. It watched the cock, the guinea fowls and all the other smaller birds gathering around, stretching out their beaks, keeping wary eyes on it, and finally it turned its back on them and ate all the bread itself.

She was thinking hard. Should she write to the poet and ask him to come to London? Before she had time to wonder whether he would be surprised to be asked, or understand that he had to be lost in Holland Park with her, she was distracted. The white peacock had spread its tail high, forming a huge fan. She approached it gently, recalling the delicacy of black sea coral, each piece a little fan, and gazed in awe at the whiteness of the peacock's own coral. It had begun to strut slowly back and forth as if it knew that its beauty made people catch their breath in wonder. Yasmin remembered what the poet had said the night before: that the peacock only displayed its feathers to attract the female.

Their conversations could not have been illusory; it was

impossible that they had never really jumped over the park wall, that he had not held her close when she told him she loved her husband and would never be unfaithful to him. He had taken her to a club afterward: she remembered the kind of chairs it had, their table, the pineapple-shaped mirrors, and exactly what the Bloody Mary tasted like when she took a sip of it to heighten her sense of elation and heard him muttering something. She had asked him what was wrong and he had replied, laughing, that he was bewitching her drink to make her love him. She had told him that she regretted not inviting him to her house in Beirut to see her beloved white plaster donkey.

It was not a dream: a dream haunts a person for a day, a week, but not a month. She wandered around big stores, looking in mirrors, trying to see herself through his eyes. He was not like other men: he noticed colors, clothes, the smallest details. She sat in Ziyad's class, trying to occupy herself by writing letters until he felt at home in the class and forgot about her. She found herself writing the poet's name. She wrote him a letter, then tore it up. She bought Lebanese magazines in the hope of finding a photo of him or one of his poems to read, in case there was an allusion to her. He was mentioning jasmine flowers for the first time: perhaps he meant her, or perhaps not. At the theater bar she wished he was with her, discussing the play like the man and woman in the corner. On the bus home she thought, If only he was sitting beside me instead of that drunk. He was real. That was why, when her husband joined her in London after a conference in the United States, she did not kiss him with any enthusiasm, or long for him as she had done in the past. She felt detached from him. She plucked up her courage and told him she loved the poet. He laughed and said with a look of tenderness on his face, "You're a dreamer. You'll never change."

She answered him silently. It can't only be a dream. Intuition sparks off love. Imaginary relationships flourish under its influence and it makes them real. It prepares the way for a meeting.

But when she was engrossed in making meals, or walking through the supermarket buying vegetables and packets and tins, or scrubbing the bath, she found it easy to separate reality from the dream. She believed the logic which told her that the romantic atmosphere of Holland Park, the white peacock, London and everything about it provided a poetic background for love: the winter, the clear skies, the cold, the green grass, the buses, the big department stores, the cinemas and theaters, the roar of noise, the untroubled atmosphere, the pigeons, the absence of war. And she was alone without a man for most of the time.

In the evenings she was once more convinced in her

mind of the reality of the dream. She tried to think of ways of meeting the poet during her stay in London. But when there was a month's ceasefire in Lebanon, Yasmin returned to Beirut. She did not think about the poet until one day she saw him approaching in the distance holding a newspaper. She smiled and continued walking.

An Unreal Life

Samr had wanted to be alone ever since they came out of their hotel into the swarming streets. If she was honest with herself, she had wanted to be alone since the plane landed.

From the moment they started walking it was like an exercise in self-defense: as the streets became narrower, the crowds grew thicker and the pack mules made walking difficult. At first they assumed that if they swerved slightly they would easily avoid them, since other people were pushing past them, dodging through the crowds, floating along like feathers. But they found themselves jumping out of the animals' way, stepping up into the doorways of the shops, which were crammed close together on either side of the street, sometimes even taking refuge inside them. The mules were loaded up with mountains of furniture, garbage, goods for sale, vegetables, even building materials. Samr's husband, who carried a tourist guide in his pocket, commented that mules took the place of cars in this ancient city, and that, like the rest of the municipal employees, they had names and numbers and received a wage for the services they provided, transporting water and refuse.

Samr received this remark with veiled scorn, but later the idea pleased her.

The narrow, twisting streets took them into a jumbled maze where the light was obscured by the crowded buildings, which met overhead, or were joined together underfoot by a tangled harvest of dried grass and weeds.

Apart from the crowds and the noise, the only things of note in these markets were the slippers, most of which were for women, lavishly decorated and in a variety of colors, reminiscent of *A Thousand and One Nights*. Whether they were on display, still in their baskets and boxes, or being examined by prospective purchasers, they appeared to be the single most important item of dress for sale.

The plan was to visit the famous old mosque, but the

crowds, and the interventions of passersby, made it difficult for her husband to study the map properly. Samr had been against the idea of the map in the first place. The moment they had gone through the archway into the old city, they had found themselves in a human beehive in a perpetual state of movement and constantly multiplying numbers, and Samr had suggested that they employ the services of one of the many boys and young men who had surrounded them and were offering—in Italian, French and English—to act as tourist guides. But her husband refused outright, as if by proposing such a thing she had insulted his intelligence and questioned his ability to manage their affairs.

They set off again through the heart of the beehive, which rose and fell with the crowd as if it lived off the movement of human beings and animals and things. The annoyance was beginning to be visible on Samr's husband's face, and he seemed to have lost the spirit of adventure that he had set out with. He looked scared too, and claustrophobic, unlike Samr, who had pressed a button in her mind that had taken her back in time. She found herself enjoying the narrow streets and the noise and the chaos as if she were a little girl again, going shopping with her grandmother. Her husband was sticking close to her now, trying to talk to her in Arabic in a vain effort to conceal his light eyes and straight, fair hair, which struck a discordant note among the curly heads. He repeated that he felt smothered by these little streets and the youths and children still streaming after them. Her response was to turn and talk to the three young men nearest them in Arabic, teasing them when they demanded to know which Arab country she came from, and whether this foreigner was her husband. They didn't move away, in spite of the crush of people and animals, and the fact that her husband was trying to stop her from walking with them, objecting to the intrusion, and pointing out the mosque on the map, insisting it was just a few meters away. Samr tried to make him see their charm and innocence, and reproved him for suspecting that their motives were purely financial.

Sure enough, they categorically refused the money that Samr held out to them on the way out of the mosque, even when she increased the amount, fearing she was offering too little, and tried to make her husband hand it to them. Then instead of disappearing back into the crowds, they invited Samr and her husband for a glass of mint tea in a cafe at the entrance to the old town.

When they all sat down, the joking and teasing suddenly ceased, and the occasion became serious. They talked in Arabic and poor French about their bleak future, and the despair of those still studying, because there were so few jobs even for graduates, and about opportunities for work and study abroad. Their enthusiasm returned as they began to discuss videos and computers.

Samr's husband's features slowly relaxed until eventually he was giving them all his attention, questioning, commenting, offering advice, while Samr was noticing the appalling state of their teeth, and the way they put their hands to their mouths to hide them whenever they laughed. Then she decided that this was a sign of embarrassment and a lack of self-confidence with strangers. She was surprised how familiar all their gestures and expressions were to her, how clearly she could see the innocence behind their sly charm.

One of the youths, whose name was Mustafa, asked her tentatively if she had any children. When she said no, their faces took on expressions of sympathy mixed with another sentiment that Samr could only guess at. This prompted her to add that they were thinking seriously about it and she was considering resigning from her job. She wanted to convey to them that she had a good relationship with her husband, and although she was always joking and laughing it didn't mean she took her marriage lightly. Since the aircraft had set her down in this city that still lived as it had done for thousands of years, she had been happy, all her senses were activated, she was full of questions, tolerant and easygoing, never focusing on one thing for long, and abounding in life and energy. These feelings didn't stem from the fact that she was on holiday, far from the clouds and the ordered reality of life in Europe. She had spent many holidays in sunny places by the sea or in the mountains, yielding to an inner calm that was more like laziness and boredom, and sleeping and eating. Now she was like a fly buzzing from one place to another, alighting on everything animate or inanimate. She realized the young men were interested in her and it reassured her to feel that she was not a stranger, fumbling her way around like the tourists, visiting all the right places and yet unable to see anything, as if the treasures were locked away in a box. When she was with them the city opened its gates wide, lit up its anterooms for her and lavished its secrets on her. She had even gotten to know the caretaker of the mosque and seen where he hid the keys. It also made her happy to know that she was still attractive to men even though she was nearly thirty-five. Attracting the opposite sex was a serious and difficult exercise in Europe because most of the time it was directed toward actually having sex. She guessed that they were not only drawn to her because it gave them the chance to flirt innocently like adolescents, although their ages ranged from twenty to twenty-five; they also saw in her and her husband a glittering pathway to the outside world that they had heard so much about. She imagined the two of them as a strange light descending suddenly on this place, which the rest of the world had overlooked and left to its own devices; it existed in a state of semidarkness and inertia, always eagerly on the lookout for the visitor who didn't see what lay behind the surface liveliness. She therefore listened gladly to their stories, and did not object to them asking her why she had married a foreigner when there must have been plenty of Arab men after her.

She felt a certain warmth toward them. She had always had a poor opinion of Arab men in general, without ever putting it to the test. And here they were, talking to her as an equal, saying whatever came into their heads without concealing anything from her husband, even if the last question had been directed at her in Arabic.

"Because I loved him," she answered, picking up the glass of sweet mint tea. She moved on to talk of generalities and let her husband do most of the talking after that. He had begun to look at her reproachfully as she became less conscientious about translating the words he missed.

When she was in her teens Samr had loved anything that came from the West: language, fashion, food, music, films, (medicaments), names, magazines and countless other things. She adored Western singers and movie actors, and even believed that she was in love with their neighbor, a Frenchman twenty years her senior, because his smile reminded her of Yves Montand's. She waited for him every morning and evening at the entrance to the building where he lived, just to hear him say, *"Bonjour, ma petite fille,"* or *"Bonsoir, ma petite fille."*

Her admiration for all things Western didn't disappear

when she left her adolescence behind. If anything it grew. She preferred going out with foreign boys, and felt at ease with their different approach, which made them seem like an extension of her favorite actors on the screen, except that they paid her an enormous amount of attention. To them she was like an exotic bird, and this was how it had been with her husband, who was working as a language teacher in the college opposite their house when she had pursued him and succeeded in catching his eye. She married him and went back with him when his contract ended, over the moon because her dream had come true.

She threw herself into all aspects of European life, including home decor. During his stay in Beirut her husband had acquired some pieces of Oriental furniture: brass trays, a mother-of-pearl table, a patterned rug. But Samr had left them wrapped up in cardboard boxes, dismissing his requests that they be allowed to see the light of day, always with the same reply: "They remind me of my grandparents' house."

She didn't share his passion for Arab music, a subject in which he had become an expert, and was not remotely interested in studying books on Arab architecture. She would even make fun of him for it: "Who's the Arab? You or me?"

Nostalgia for her roots came back to her at odd moments—for example, when a Turkish musician played a *re-*

bec in the street near her office—but she never thought of doing anything about it until she saw a film on television about Yemen made by a European woman journalist. Samr was not merely captivated by the country's rugged beauty and its customs; the film opened doors for her that had been stuck fast for years, and she remembered her own country with feeling, and could see a certain area vividly in her mind because of its similarity to the pictures on the television.

She realized why she had been obsessed recently with countries like Nepal and Bhutan and Kashmir. She had thought it was a reaction to Europe's frostiness, to its tidy, monotonous reality, to the predictability of life there. The real reason had eluded her, which was that she had begun to concern herself with the essence of things and spend large amounts of time thinking about why and how things were as they were. This had happened since she had started living in Europe and people had asked her about her country and that part of the world, and she had craftily changed the subject, because she knew nothing about it. Eventually she had begun to read foreign books about the area, since the books that she found in the only Arab bookshop in the city were irrelevant: they discussed the interpretation of dreams, or gave advice to female university students in Arab countries. She began ordering books from her own country and visiting the section in the museum devoted to antiquities from the area, and she became addicted to Arabic music, discovering the best of it, thanks to the fact that this was what Western musicians had chosen to hear.

Her husband welcomed her return, since he had been attracted to her mainly because she was an Arab. He liked saying her name, and liked what it meant: the beautiful and convivial and exciting side of the night. He liked the way she spoke and the color of her skin, which, according to him, meant that human beings had really existed for thousands and thousands of years, and were born from the soil and colored by the sun.

He was asking now if they could go back to the hotel, as he'd been told that sunset was one of the nicest times to have a cup of tea on the balcony. But Samr was still revolving like a spinning top, her thoughts in a whirl and her eyes darting everywhere. She'd always put her lack of energy down to her low blood pressure, but now she realized it was because she had lost her enthusiasm for life.

She went reluctantly back to the hotel with him, tearing herself away from the cafe. She listened to the youths commenting on the women and girls going in and out of the public baths opposite and telling exaggerated stories, and felt like one of them. She seemed to be missing a time in her life she had never known. She guessed her husband wanted to go back to the hotel so that he could be alone with her, and things could be normal again. He had surely begun to feel that she was interested in everything but him. She had even stopped translating the jokes for him.

This showed that she was detaching herself from him, but she would return to him when they went home. There was a gap in her relationship with him that she had only stumbled into here. She tried to push this new feeling into a corner of her mind and interrogated herself again, refusing to accept that it revealed anything complicated. It was simply that she wanted to be alone in these surroundings, away from the Orientalist spirit that had characterized him in their excursions so far. Although he was able to understand this culture and had studied it in depth, his heart remained immune to it, as if it were mummified like a pharoah, protected from life and even from death. The difference, which had been the magic drawing her and binding her to him, had begun to change here to impatience and exasperation at having to explain things and dispel misunderstandings. She tried to clear away the boulders of resentment and incomprehension that had begun to accumulate and interfere with their enjoyment, especially when they were in the mosque.

When she stepped off the narrow street, she had not expected to see a big piece of the sky descending into the vastness of the mosque, and its blues and whites and mauves and pinks forming a mosaic that shifted and changed according to the position of the sun and the direction of the breeze.

They entered a courtyard seething with life and vigor. Men doing their ritual ablutions were jostled by children anxious to play in the fountain and sail their paper boats in the water, while the women sat as if they were on a social visit, at home in the heart of this space, away from the gloom of their houses, chewing gum, cracking seeds between their teeth and drinking tea from thermoses.

Tears rained down Samr's cheeks. Her husband examined the mosaic, appraising the restorations and comparing it with Alhambra, seeing nothing beyond the artistic achievement.

Samr restrained herself. She couldn't persuade herself that this difference which had brought them together was what was now driving them apart. She had to be more honest and acknowledge that his presence was a hindrance to her because she wanted to become immersed in this city on her own. She needed to think up some excuses, and from now on she mustn't let her husband see her impatience and exasperation.

The following day she persuaded him to let her go shopping alone with one of the boys because if he came with her the prices would shoot up like the mercury in a thermometer. Mustafa was the one who went with her; he was the linchpin of the group.

Samr almost bounded along. She was alone and free, to shop, to stare, to bargain and haggle. She bought leather goods at rock-bottom prices once she discovered Mustafa's bargaining skills and learned from them. All she had left to buy was henna. Mustafa led her in and out of the alleyways until they reached an open square where two huge sycamores sheltered the vendors' barrows from the sun. She was delighted to see this open space, which was almost a rarity, being in a public road rather than hidden away behind closed doors like most of the space in the city. She clutched the dried henna leaves, finding it hard to believe that the powder that tinged hair red came from pale green leaves like these. Mustafa greeted a youth buying a juice from a street stall. Samr noticed the two of them looking at her as she sniffed the henna. She smiled at them and picked up the bags containing herbs and clay for strengthening hair, which Mustafa insisted on taking from her. He introduced her to his friend, Jalal, and the three of them walked on together in the direction of a building at the far end of the square. Mustafa volunteered the information that it was a historic building, which Jalal was in charge of restoring.

When she was sightseeing with her husband they had been shown a number of places that were supposed to be out of bounds to tourists, and in the process of being restored, but these had been no more impressive than unlit building sites. In the garden of this ruined mansion there were cats stretched out in blissful indolence in the sun and orange trees with fruit on them, glowing like lamps. She would have rather stayed outside than visited yet another gloomy building site, where not even the heaps of rubble and dirt gave any hint that the building would be returned to its former glory or justify its renewed existence. Besides, the sense of abandonment and neglect surrounding these places, lying there like hidden pearls, made her sad rather than angry and eager to act, like her husband.

She was taken aback by Mustafa's friend's coolness. He was quite unlike Mustafa and the other young men, who had pleasant, open expressions and had been welcoming to Samr and her husband. He was indifferent, self-contained and didn't even ask her what country she came from or express surprise at her knowledge of Arabic. He played with a bunch of keys as he continued talking to Mustafa and ignoring her existence. Finally she asked him if she was intruding, but he merely shook his head without comment, while Mustafa laughed and made some self-conscious remark about his friend being dumb.

Jalal went toward the stairs, which Samr knew in advance would be in complete darkness. She found it hard to adjust to the gloom, and she didn't want to let Mustafa help her, as he had on previous occasions, by taking her hand or guiding her by the elbow. Jalal continued climbing even though she was eager to look in some of the rooms they were passing. He seemed to be used to these requests from tourists as he continued to mutter indistinctly at intervals that it would still be there later, and nothing was going to disappear.

When they came out onto the roof, Samr was entranced. Her heart began to thump as it often did when she was flying in her dreams, and she soared out over the colored rooftops.

She flew above the dusty, ordinary buildings, above the roofs with green and blue tiles, the colors of lapis lazuli and emerald, above the high white domes crowned with copper, above fortresslike buildings and colored circles—strawberry, mustard, wine and indigo. Men were dipping cloth in these pools of color, then squeezing it out, and in the same, open square other men gathered wearing velvet skullcaps and *jallabiyyas*, looking like grasshoppers with their limbs stuck out at various angles.

She flew in pursuit of the narrow, snaking streets, and understood from this height why someone had thought of building the city in this way: not to delight the eye, but deliberately to conceal its maze of streets, which belonged to the veiled women of the past, enabling them to stride from one doorstep to another and disappear through ordinary doors into big, roomy houses, while men stole glances at them from shop doorways.

Tears welled up in Samr's eyes again and she had to

remind herself sternly that it was only a couple of days before she went back home. She would soon be living a normal life and this visit would become a memory. But how could she leave it all and go back to Europe? She knew she was letting her imagination run away with her: it would be impossible to live in this city. But she couldn't tear herself away from it and was oblivious to the mounting impatience of Mustafa and his friend, who had ceased to respect her silence and begun chatting again, taking no notice of her vague, distracted air.

She didn't move an inch until Mustafa raised his voice to remind her that he was still there, but she refused to feel embarrassed, or leave just because they wanted her to. She knew she'd regret it if she did: in the past she had agreed to let go of feelings that she had then never experienced again. Rather than agreeing to go, she suggested that Mustafa could leave her there if he was busy and pick her up later. She asked his friend if she could stay and he had no alternative but to nod his head, telling Mustafa with a glance toward her shopping that he would walk her back to her hotel. To her surprise, Mustafa agreed instantly, which made her think that her splendor must have faded in his eyes, then she told herself that he had a life too.

Immediately after Mustafa left, she managed to disengage herself from the city's embrace as if she were leaving a child safe in bed.

She went down the stairs with Jalal into a small room with unremarkable mosaic tiles and a whitewashed floor, then ducked after him through a small window set in the wall. She suddenly wondered for a moment if she should be on her guard. She didn't know this man and having to bend and twist her body to go after him made her uneasy, but when she stood up on the other side she drew in her breath in amazement.

Her life outside ceased to be real. Reality was here. The rose-colored stained-glass shapes in the ceiling cast a pink mist over the tall pillars in the center of the vast room, the geometrical patterns and the enameled friezes on the walls, the chandeliers, and the glass vessels displayed in wooden latticework cabinets. Samr sat down on a lone chair to absorb what was in front of her. The silence all around her enveloped her suddenly. The room was like a holy book that had never been opened. The small stained-glass shapes on the ceiling preserved the light of the past. Samr closed her eyes. Nothing disturbed the silence except the echoing of Jalal's footsteps, which were soon absorbed, leaving only the rosy mist—the remains of the sunlight of past days, which had stolen through the stained glass and preferred to linger in this calm.

She wanted to live here forever and pictured herself as a woman from another age, emerging from her bath and beginning to prepare for the late afternoon, for sunset, for the evening, in an era when each hour of the day was precious and had its own ceremonies. At some point time had come to a halt in this room and she partook of its stillness, gazing at the mosaic in a trance. Then she shifted in her chair, wishing vaguely that she had a glass of mint tea, and holding the amber perfume on her wrist up to her mouth and nose.

But the dry, unemotional behavior of Mustafa's friend was spoiling the serenity of these moments, which were also dense with ambiguous feelings. He moved between a table in the corner, where he had spread out his blueprints, and another where he had put a thermos, a teapot and a bunch of mint. She tried to ignore his movements so that the place would remain outside space and time, and did not understand why his presence was becoming so intrusive. She wanted to be on good terms with him so that there was nothing to disrupt her sense of harmony. She asked him suddenly if she would be able to rent a house like the one they were in.

"Why?"

"So I could come here for a few months in the year."

"Why?"

She felt embarrassed because she didn't know the answer, but she could see herself reclining on a sofa in these spacious surroundings. She answered in a low voice, as if she didn't want him to hear her properly: "So that I can live with this beauty around me!"

"Is your man going to come with you?"

I don't know, she thought. But she said, "My husband? I don't think so."

"It shouldn't be a problem. What price do you want to pay? What kind of house do you have in mind? With or without a *gharsa?*"

"Gharsa?"

"Jardin."

"A house with a garden."

"We can go and have a look. It shouldn't be a problem."

Samr fidgeted uneasily, regretting that she had become so quickly embroiled, but this regret was soon buried under a surge of confidence. He began to show an interest in her for the first time, asking her if she liked the city, what job she did in Europe, what country she came from, whether Mustafa had taken her to this or that place, and he promised to bring her henna from his mother—genuine henna that his mother prepared herself—and said she must visit their house, because she'd like it, especially the garden. Then he began rolling a cigarette, assuring her that it was an ordinary one, but if she wanted to smoke hash . . . Samr laughed, and shook her head. He took a few drags on the cigarette, then let it dangle from his lips and started beating his chest as if he were playing a drum, varying the rhythm by switching between the flat of his hand and his fist, and humming and whistling in time to the beat. Samr was afraid of the way she had started to feel—like a tender plant, its stem bending as it searched for water and sunshine—and she forced herself to stand up.

He looked at his watch and asked her if she wanted to go. Then he added hesitantly, "We can talk for a bit first if you like."

But she started to move with slow, heavy steps. As he bent down to pick up the shopping, she thought he brushed her skirt with his hand. Then he did it again, and she was sure. He straightened up and stood facing her and leaned forward to kiss her. She didn't move away or resist. He put a hand on her breast. Again she didn't resist, but returned his kiss with passion. She opened her eyes and saw the mosaic walls, then closed them again, soaring through the darkness until her lips and his, and the light and color around her, and even the image of her husband and the group of young men all became part of a single sensation.

She was roused from her stupor each time he led her into a different movement. At first she would be nervous, then grow accustomed to it, and the rosy glow would return and she would close her eyes again and fly off into the dark.

She didn't look at him when he got up, saying he would make some tea. Instead she thought about her husband. She pictured him sitting with Mustafa and the rest of the group, chatting around the pool in the evenings, with his maps and the additional information about the city spread out all around him. She stirred restlessly and tried to calm herself by smoothing out the creases in her long skirt. Then she forgot about her husband as she watched Jalal pouring the tea, and he was like the finishing touch to the awe-inspiring surroundings.

She wondered desperately whether she would have the chance to see him alone again before she left, or whether she should stay on a few days after her husband, or come back in a month's time.

He handed her the tea. She took the glass from him in complete silence, but smiled broadly at him and he returned the smile.

She thought about Mustafa and was on the point of begging him not to tell Mustafa and the rest of the group. This was not only in case her husband should hear about it, but for their sakes too. She didn't want them to have a confused image of her. It was as if she wanted to protect them. He looked at his watch. She looked at hers, and said without conviction, "I ought to be getting back to the hotel."

He jumped to his feet as if he had been waiting for her to say this, and took the glass of tea from her, although she hadn't touched it.

He must be on edge, she thought. Afraid of Mustafa. And of my husband.

She hoped he would say something to her. She braced herself, but he was preoccupied with the keys.

She went in front of him downstairs and he took hold of her hand. This reassured her in a way, although she noticed she was no longer as desperate for his touch as she had been when she was sitting staring at him smoking and playing the drums on his chest. The moment they stepped outside, the mosaic walls and rosy mist disappeared and were replaced by the roar of the street. She stood a few paces away from him while he locked the door. She was back in the noise and chaos. She saw people rushing, dawdling, calling to one another, walking along in silence. She had come back to life again. She read a flashing neon sign, and noticed a man looking at her.

Jalal turned the key a couple of times in the lock, then bolted the door, and she caught herself staring at him as if she were seeing him for the first time. She tried with difficulty to connect this image of him with the man who had been inside the house with her. It was like trying to unite fire and water. The man standing in front of her had different eyes, a different physique, even a different voice, and she couldn't believe that she had been lying with him a short time before. She found herself looking up at the windows in case a different man was looking down at her, his hand raised in a farewell salute. Perhaps he was waiting for her now, while the youth in front of her was opening the gate for her to leave. When she turned back to him she half expected to find that he had been a figment of her imagination.

The crowds in the street made her apprehensive: she was afraid she might see Mustafa and the others, and her husband, and then wished she could see them. She wanted to disappear as she and Jalal made for the hotel, and was relieved that he wasn't holding her hand. She felt as if she had weights attached to her feet, and summoned up the courage to tell him that she would write to him in a few months to let him know when she wanted to rent a house. He nodded agreeably and her anxiety grew: she had only said this to prompt him to leave. It wasn't going to be easy to get rid of him. How could she explain to him that he had provided the finishing touch to the place, but she was never going to see him again? He was behaving awkwardly himself. Was he waiting for a chance to continue the relationship begun in the paradise house?

As they approached the bright lights of the hotel, she grew more fearful and he grew more embarrassed. When the hotel was clearly visible he stopped. She stopped beside him, the answers and excuses almost bursting out from between her lips. But she was aware of him speaking to her in French for the first time: "Help me. I don't have the money to go to university. There's no money in this job."

Samr was so completely taken aback that she couldn't move, and was forced to remain looking into his eyes. It was as if a heavy bird had suddenly landed on her head and was constricting her neck movements, but she managed to hear him repeating in French: "Will you help me?"

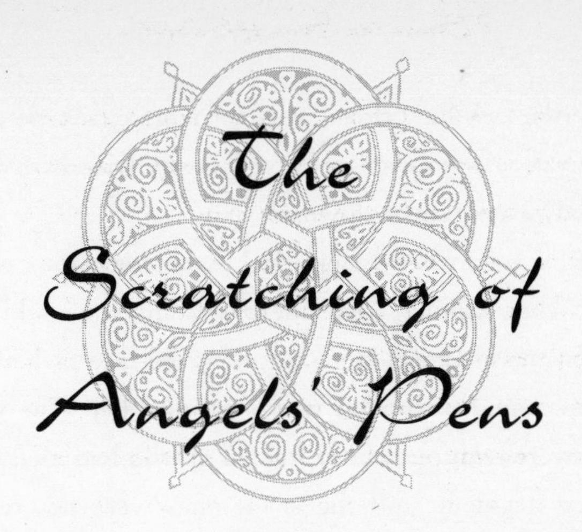

The Scratching of Angels' Pens

Don't use the jug with a long spout to do your ablutions! Don't wash your face with scented soap! Don't admire the moon! Don't bleach your sheets! You mustn't raise your voice above a whisper, especially when there's a man present, even if he's in the next room! If you want to clear your throat or sigh, shut yourself in the bathroom! Don't forget, three months and ten days, or preferably four months, you stay in the house, day and night. Even if you're unwell, don't go out. But if you get worse, call me and I'll go with you. Keep away from your flashy friends. Don't eat nice food! Don't smell flowers!

Shadia sat in her black clothes between two rows of women, some wailing, some silent, wishing she could be left alone for one moment. Her pale, haggard face picked up all the glances and unspoken words around her. The wailing women were relations of her husband, who had died following a car accident, and the silent ones were her relations and acquaintances of her family.

She wished she was still with him in the hospital. Although he had finally slipped through her fingers, those days had been beautiful compared with what she was going through now. She had him to herself in that room. For hours in the daytime and during the night she sat with him, watching him, unable to believe that their dialogue had become limited to the brief moment when he would move slightly and she would rise from where she had been sitting at his feet, massaging them, and touch his face. Then he would signal to her with his eyes, his forehead, his nose—it was hard to know which—and she would rest her cheek against his and feel the dampness of the saliva that trickled from the corners of his mouth. Perhaps he wanted to kiss her. He muttered words she didn't understand, then focused his eyes on her as if he were giving her all he possessed.

Sometimes he showed her the tip of his tongue and she dropped a kiss on his mouth and brought her hair close to him, putting a lock of it in his palm and closing his fingers around it, rejoicing when she felt him pressing on it. She spent hours like this, motionless at his side, looking at the veins on his hand, at his fingers clutching her black hair. To her disappointment, he would always drift back into a deep sleep. But after a while she was thankful he slept—perhaps it would rest him and make him better. She would sit without moving until one of the nurses came in, and Shadia would be glad of her company. All the nurses admired her boldness and devotion.

Her little daughter was clinging to her now, but this was no consolation to her. She was being smothered under a thick blanket of whispered remarks, and it was impossible to escape, for the talk was now about more than the jug and the moon and unperfumed soap: "Come on! Given a bit of time, she'll go back to her first husband and start bringing up this daughter of hers again. See, the Almighty's taken His revenge."

When Shadia heard this she hid her face in her hands. To stop them intruding on her privacy, she bowed her head and retreated within herself so that she was alone, as she had wanted to be all along. She abandoned herself to her passionate thoughts, conjuring up his smell, especially the smell of his neck and under his arms, his smell before he went to sleep and when he woke up, and before and after shaving. Eventually she worked around to the smell of the first kiss. She found herself delaying, hesitating, uncertain where she wanted to freeze her thoughts so as to enjoy them for the maximum possible time. But then she let them run on, again reliving the moment he first entered her, which in its intensity surpassed all that followed, even the ecstasy, because it was the focal point, dissolving the agony that had been eating away at her: her sorrow at leaving her daughter, her horror at the idea that her lover would marry somebody else before she could get away from her husband, her fear of facing her family and the neighbors.

As soon as she felt him right inside her, she was sure she had been created for this moment. She closed her eyes, savoring the peace of mind that she thought had been taken away from her for good.

But they didn't leave her alone with him now, any more than they had done before, when she ran away with him and they had pursued her with violent talk and messages and threats. Their voices reached her, and she felt they were working her in their hands like a piece of dough, especially the women on her family's side. The others were mulling over their loss with enormous anguish, which made them accuse her of being the reason for God's vengeance on him.

Her aunt was trying to make her change her name back to Rashida, "the wise," for Shadia—which means "the singer"—symbolized his era, as he was the one who had given her the name, and now she had to go back to being wise . . . and don't do your ablutions with the tin jug because the long spout will remind you of men, and you shouldn't look at the moon because it's male, and . . .

Shadia kept her eyes determinedly shut, lost in her memories of how he had smelled, the way he had touched every part of her, even her toes, sensing him all around her. Then her feelings took off in another direction as she heard the women discussing, more audibly now, how she would be forced to go back to her previous husband this time, straight after the seclusion period, and how she would be moved to her brother's house in the meantime. She found herself blessing death, deciding that she too would die. She closed her eyes and held her breath. She wanted to suffocate. She squeezed her chest, as if she could wrench her heart out of place. However, she remained fully conscious, and happened to glance down at her healthy hands. Her longing for him must be interfering with her grief and giving her strength and vitality. She willed herself to die again, picturing him cold and lifeless, as if he had never known her. She was startled when her aunt forced her head upward, pried her clenched hands away from her body and pushed her daughter toward her, hoping to oblige Shadia to take the child in her arms.

"Bear up!" her aunt ordered her briskly. "It's God's law. Dust to dust." Then she went on, "You must repent. Return to the fold. Defeat the keeper of hell's furnaces by showing him you've slipped through his fiery fingers. What more could the believer desire? Naturally, the angels' pens will cross your bad deed off the slate if you return to your first husband. They'll be even surer of you if you look up into the sky at night when you're dozing off to sleep—after your period of seclusion, of course—wait until you see a shooting star, then close your eyes, say, 'There is no god but God,' and repent. This star will hear and hurry to curse Satan, who tempted you to commit adultery. Repent so that you can go to heaven and see 'the ground gleaming white like silver and pearls, the earth made of musk, the saffron plants, the trees with alternating leaves of silver and gold.' "[1]

Shadia's eyelids did not even flicker while her aunt was speaking: she was still trying to die. But one sentence penetrated the gloom, and gave her a glimmer of hope.

[1] Sayings attributed to the Prophet Muhammad by Imam Ibn al-'Abbas. From *Kitab al-Isra' wa'l-Mi'raj* ("The Book of Muhammad's night journey to the seventh heaven"), Sudan, n.d.

"Heaven is the place where all couples are reunited," said her aunt.

But as quickly as Shadia had rushed to greet the words, she backed away from them. "Will I meet my first husband or my second?" she demanded.

Her question, asked in a heartfelt rush of despair and terror, rolled over ears that had never heard an amorous whisper, a kind word or a beautiful melody, and was buried in hearts that knew only frustration and anxiety.

Her aunt lashed out at her with loathing, disregarding the rest of the company, as if her chance for revenge had come at last. "You've lived exactly as you pleased and dragged us through the mud, and we're still paying for it. If you repent, at least we'll get some benefit. But you want to guarantee your afterlife as well. You scheming whore!" She paused and then burst out again with venomous delight, "Your first husband, of course."

As Shadia's world fell apart, she heard one of the women asserting that God forgives all a woman's sins except adultery. Shadia closed her eyes, recollecting what she had read in her teens about the terrors of the afterlife, about "women hanging by their hair in the infernal zaqoum tree and having boiling water poured over them till their flesh came off in strips, because they'd taken medicine to get rid of their unwanted children," and "women whose faces had been burnt and whose tongues lolled out onto their chests, because they had asked their husbands to divorce them for no reason."[2]

Too bad. Shadia nodded her head calmly, accepting her fate. "I don't care," she said, and rid herself of two images: herself in bed with her first husband, and lying with him on the pearly white ground of Paradise.

[2] See note 1.

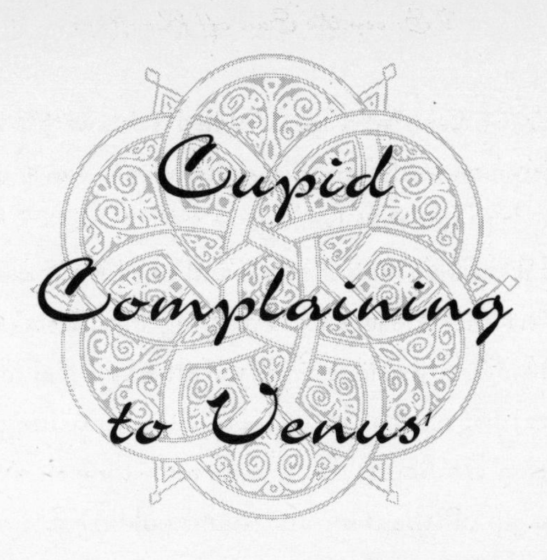

Cupid Complaining to Venus[1]

I woke up this morning thinking I was a tin can stuck away on a shelf, wanting to be picked up by a pair of hands and opened so that some of the air trapped inside could escape. It wasn't the spring urging me to open up even though it has always stirred animals and birds to cover thousands of miles for the sake of sex. No. It was my night-dress.

[1] The title of a painting by Lucas Cranach (1472–1553).

Why do I keep wearing it when I know I'll be disappointed as usual in the morning after sex? Now I only have to picture it to get that feeling.

I pull it off and fling it away and put on a dress suitable for cleaning the house and scrubbing bathrooms. Perhaps this will bring me back to reality. But I still feel like a fruit stone discarded on the sidewalk: a mango, my luscious flesh sucked from its fibers by a voracious tongue. I pick the nightdress up off the floor and stand holding it. I should be grateful it's this ivory color, not rose pink. Rose pink would be too much.

I know that color of pink which promises uninterrupted passion, but it's a color you don't see anymore: maybe the people who mix fabric dyes have never seen pomegranate seeds, and you can be sure that nobody examines the color of a woman's nipple anymore except the doctor.

But there must be women like me looking for it, and if they find it unfortunately it's in nightdresses that have seen better days in secondhand-clothes shops, and bras and corsets that depend on more than plastic bones to give them shape: they were made for women like my mother's friend whose breasts used to be the object of regular attacks by me and my brother. I mean we would sit on her knees as close as possible to the two big mountains and she would fend us off, laughing until her whole body shook, including the two mountains, and we were happy when they touched us. She told my mother of the salesgirl who stuck her head in the cup of a bra she'd been looking at and said, "This one's the right size for you."

I forgot to say that this color has a smell like a powder puff, the smell of roses. And I also forgot to describe its silky feel as it slips through your fingers like quicksilver.

I look at myself in the mirror, so disappointed and sour, and vow that this will be the last time I wake up in this state.

I didn't think about liberating my body until I was on a summer holiday with my friend Muna. Sex began cropping up in our conversations all the time and dominated our thoughts as we sat in our white summer cottons under the gentle sun, arranging our long hair, or appeared in the restaurant in all our finery after a long day's preparation of our bodies: stretching them out under a layer of hot wax that picked up even the downy little face hairs so the surface of the skin was smooth as pearls, surrendering them to the masseuse's hands, soaking them in frangipani milk, giving them a siesta, dressing them in underwear so soft it almost slipped off the skin, then sitting them down to wait and enjoy more conversations about sex, and fidget with lust. Even so, they showed no interest in flirting with the other guests in the hotel, quite the opposite: they couldn't wait to be alone with the men they pictured waiting in bed for them, naked and scarcely able to contain their impatience.

Meanwhile, we dawdled, fueling our desires and tantalizing these creatures of our bodies' fantasies. But this intimate atmosphere changed at once when Muna began describing how she felt when she was with someone who understood what her body wanted: how she became like an unweaned baby content to lie back and suck on its pacifier, daydreaming about the flood of warmth and nourishment to come.

"But that kind of desire isn't always there," she added. If she hadn't said that, my throat would have exploded with the pulse that was beating there and preventing me from speaking. "It's not always like that. I've had some disappointments too. There was one man who brought his big heavy hand down on my breast like a flyswatter and tweaked my nipples as if he was picking dust off a curtain. And I remember another who couldn't work out where the well was in spite of the wetness all around. He whispered to me, demanding to know if I was normal, did I have a hole? And he hung on to my hair the whole time, as if he was scared he'd lose his balance and fall off! And of course there was the one who began to groan and sigh and gasp for breath and had his eyes shut. I thought he was having a heart attack, I didn't realize it was just passion, so I sent for the doctor!"

We laughed together, her laughter submerging mine because she saw them as she talked, and then her laughter silenced me. Suddenly there was this pulse beating in my throat again and it squirted out creatures that tried to throttle me as I listened to her saying how she used to rage like a fire, keeping the men off her with her hands, her tongue; scolding, mocking, angry as she laid down her terms for sex. And I was still behaving like a donkey, going down a road against my will, and on top of that, reassuring whoever was riding me that this was the ideal way, the way I'd always dreamed of, sometimes going to the lengths of hiding the hooves that had been bloodied by the sharp stones on the bumpy road.

When I owned up to this, Muna was shocked to the core. She had always known me as a mistress of manipulation and deceit, a woman who took a thirsty man to water and led him back thirstier still, plucked words from a mute's mouth, pulled out an eyelash even if there were no lashes there. Had I still managed to fall into the trap of my own cunning? Here I was complaining to her, like little Cupid to tall, sublime Venus, that I'd been stung by a nest of bees on my face and hands and chest, because my face was turned to the wall and I was lying on my front with one arm underneath me and the other hanging down desolately in space. All this just so that the joiner could try and make a hole for the screw to go into.

Muna stroked my hair and twisted my curls around her fingers, just as Venus must have done to Cupid, and tried to soothe away my sadness and irritation with wise words that were addressed to the depths of my soul rather than being designed to instruct me on what my tongue could do.

"But why do I have to teach him how to kiss me? How to make love to me? Why doesn't he—?"

"Shhh. Listen." She wouldn't let me talk at all, being rational just like Venus, and I was following her advice as if I had no choice. Her eyes were fixed on me, following me wherever I went. She controlled me as if invisible strings were attached to every part of my body and I only moved when she jerked them.

My lover and I watched the video Muna had picked out for me. I wasn't relaxing and enjoying it as I was meant to. Instead I was searching for clues like a detective, wanting to grab hold of the tongue as it moved up and down, in complete control. I watched intently, wishing that one shot would last longer, or another could have been in close-up. When my lover turned his attention to the dish of sliced carrots, I felt the strings working my feet, my head, my whole body and I wanted to make him turn back to the television for fear the golden opportunity would be missed. I saw that he was shaking his head in disgust. "Did you see how wide they were opening their mouths? Thank God I'm not that guy eating the woman's tongue. It's revolting! It distorts the shape of her lips, makes her look grotesque."

This was only the first stone to come rolling down the

mountainside. Others followed: "That's way over the top!" and "Why can't they be satisfied with portraying sex as it is?"

When I repeated this last remark to Muna, she stopped pulling my strings and acted on her own behalf. She gave a little shiver and clapped her hands. "If only he could see me making love! He'd take it back and understand that what he saw on the video was one hundred percent realistic!"

She wouldn't let me despair and gave me some more movies, assuring me that he was the man I'd been looking for, because smell was the elixir of sex and I was always excited by his smell; even the thought of it drove me crazy. She told me how she'd paid a huge sum to have her lover's scent manufactured artificially and distilled into a little bottle, so that she could sniff it and load herself up with it when she wanted things to flow with another man.

I watched the new videos with my lover; they had scenes depicting the five senses, as if the lovers' creator had given them life and immediately withdrawn his breath from them, leaving them in this raw state to take in smells, to be numbed, to plunge deep into the images before them and take on their colors and absorb their tastes until they became the tastes themselves. The woman lay down and spread her thighs like airplane wings; her waist was the aircraft's belly, her breasts its propellers, her pussy the engine. She soared away without leaving the ground.

I followed her movements breathlessly, wishing that I too could fly without leaving the ground.

"How beautiful it was!" I said.

"Did you notice? Just like we do it sometimes," he said.

"Wasn't it a new way?" I pretended innocence.

"That! It's the most classic of all!" he asserted like a scientist in a laboratory.

I swallowed and bit my bottom lip and wondered if this means I was losing my nerve. Then the words come involuntarily. "No. We've never done it like that," I said firmly.

"Your memory seems a bit rusty."

"No. I haven't forgotten. I don't remember opening my legs like that."

"What? Are you really saying that you've never opened your legs!"

"I mean I've never opened my legs the way the woman in the video did."

"Opening the legs is opening the legs. No two ways about it."

"You're wrong. There is a difference. Those legs opened like a pair of scissors."

"You're ungrateful! That's all there is to it. Ungrateful!" he said irritably.

"Did you hear me saying anything except that I've never opened my legs like it showed on the video?"

"You're ungrateful. So ungrateful. Shall I remind you

how you moaned? Shall I remind you how much you enjoyed it?"

"I just said I didn't open my legs like the actress."

Now he was shouting. "You don't know when you're well off. Naturally you've forgotten that I'm always ready. You're the one who's tired or not feeling well."

Now I was shouting too. "I don't open my legs like her. That's all I'm saying."

"And I'm telling you that you must have forgotten. That you don't know how lucky you are. Ask your imagination. Perhaps it would have been better if I'd made love to that. It might remember how strong I was, how exuberant."

"But . . . all I wanted—"

"Tell me which of your friends has a man like me, with my strength . . ."

Later, when my lover, whom I love, wanted me to have a glass of wine with him, I refused. I told him there was a magnetic force in my blood, pulling my energies down between my legs, while wine went to my head, and I wanted all the ecstasy for the black lace at the center, the focus of all feelings, crude and sublime. The moment I found myself underneath the man whom I love and who loves me, I spread my legs just like a crab. If crabs kept their legs together they wouldn't be able to move around and find food; to put it bluntly, they'd die.

But my lover bundled me up and returned me to the

fetal position. I was squeezing my eyelashes tight shut—he'd once said they were like fans—so that I couldn't see what my heart was feeling. I couldn't believe that one of my ears—which he'd said were as sweet and tempting as cotton candy—could be pressed so hard against the pillow, while the other strained to hear a single passionate word. When my arm went numb under the weight of my body, I tried in vain to extricate it with the other arm. To counter my disillusion, I tried to convince myself that I should be satisfied with feeling the way I did about my thighs. Letting my mind wander, I pictured them as two smooth slopes that the traveler had to climb in order to find the Venus flytrap, the welcoming flower that would give him squeezing, sucking kisses and spread its nectar around about him.

My thoughts must have given me the energy to turn toward my lover, not to complain this time, but to offer him my face or, to be more exact, my nose, the one out of all the body's orifices through which the spirit enters and leaves. This was to remind him that when we slept together it was like a continuation of our whispered conversations, our shared smell, the looks we gave each other. The whole of him had to enter me, not just a part of him, enter me holding the thread of water that would irrigate every corner of me, all that is me: my heart, which wants and desires him, and my mind likewise; two bodies in one soul or two souls in one body. So I stretched before him like a cat, but as always he shut my legs again with an unconscious gesture, as if he were folding a deck chair, and rolled me up like a ball of wool, pinning me in with my arms. I was squeezing my eyelids shut again to block out what was happening between my legs. I noticed he had summoned all his strength, and he was racing along like a man on horseback, every sinew and bone and drop of blood in his body hell-bent on winning the race.

I took my head in my hands and drew my limbs in tightly like a mummy. Later I unwrapped myself and went to the local arts center, where I was to give a reading. I felt myself relaxing as I settled myself comfortably to read a short story.

There was a woman in a village in the country who used to leave her mud-brick house every morning wearing a black headcover fixed with a colored rope and a translucent face veil which left only her eyes free. As she stepped out she was well aware that the sight of veiled women sets hearts ablaze, because the imagination cannot rest until it has seen the whole face. She made her way through the fields and trees, carrying an earthenware water jar on her hip, which looked like a man resting comfortably in the hollow of her waist. As soon as she got to the river, she put the jar down at the water's edge, raised her veil, and splashed water over her neck and face, then under the arms of her dress. She filled the water jar and went back but this time she took the route through the village. She balanced the jar on her head and began swinging her hips from side to side and sticking out her breasts and moving them to the right and to the left. Buttocks, breast. Buttocks, breast. Until the men's eyes were fastened on her and their sighs followed her, as she walked firmly on, saying to herself, "Even if you make me wear a veil and hide my face from the world, you can't hide my body."

Soon afterward this woman married a man whose imagination wouldn't rest until he had seen the face which complemented the eyes and lashes and beautifully arched brows. This was why, when they had a daughter who was the spitting image of her mother, her father wouldn't let her hide her face behind a veil.

I stopped reading and let my eyes wander over the audience. I knew my black, low-cut dress, dark eyes and skin and Rita Hayworth hair, long rippling waves the color of aubergines, attracted their attention more than my reading. Once I felt they were listening, I recrossed my legs, pursed my lips, made the warmth ooze from my voice and finished reading my story.

This girl refused to help her mother with the housework. When she was reprimanded she exploded in anger: "What right have you to call me lazy? If you knew what happens to me when I do housework you'd bless my disobedience. Every time I go up and down stairs my breasts roll from side to side and my hips sway and I get aroused. Every time I rest against the sink to wash the dishes the hardness of the concrete arouses me. When I knead the dough my bottom shakes and makes my pussy vibrate. When I bend down to scrub the floor, the sweat collects between my thighs and makes me excited. When I hollow out the zucchini with the vegetable corer it makes me think of fucking."

In no time at all her excuses were making the rounds of young and old and making people toss and turn in bed. Then a young man came knocking on the door in the middle of the night, asking to marry her, and the next day they were married, and she bore him a daughter as beautiful as the full moon. The girl grew up and followed the same path as her mother and grandmother, beset with feelings and desires. But she made a big mistake when she found herself with her lover and wanted to spread her thighs like a leaf opening as the light touches it.

I stopped reading to have a sip of water, confident that among the audience I had found someone who would take my face in his hands and let me lie the way I wanted to. I saw him even though my eyes had not left the page. But his eyes grazed my skin, and started heating up my blood.

Qut al-Qulub

The silver rays cast by the full moon over the village of Kawkabana were unusually bright, because the village was higher even than the clouds. It appeared to have grown by itself on the summit of the mountain, for how could the clay and earth and little colored glass windows have been transported up there unless a goat had carried them in its teeth? And even a goat would have needed some kind of track; a human being without shoes or sandals could never have done it. All the same, this village was there, carved into the rocky mountain, making the summit into a complete circle. It was as if the mountain had enlisted the help of jinns to build a place which was so inaccessible that only those who loved it would make the effort to reach it. Every stone was polished and arranged with regard to its size and color and the result was an ornament of incomparable beauty.

When the moon was full the women were overcome with happiness, eagerly anticipating the things they would do—fill the paraffin lamps, and stay up late strolling around well into the night now that they no longer needed to be afraid of scorpions and snakes. They would set off to listen to songs and chew qat in the yards of their mud-brick houses, accompanying one another on drums and tambourines, all happy except Layla, who used to say, "Every time there's a full moon, it reminds me that life is short."

But the village women who practiced magic were convinced that the silver moonlight spoiled their witchcraft and waited until the moon waned or was completely hidden by the clouds before they began again to prepare amulets, which were always written under cover of darkness, or bury locks off doors in the night (this was done to open up a woman's tubes). The moonlight not only laid bare their plans and destroyed their potions but seemed to exert its authority over all human powers. Only the magician Qut al-Qulub disagreed with them: she swore that she could work magic only by moonlight. She always claimed that its silver beams penetrated curtains, stonework, wood shutters and glass windows and shook her awake if she was asleep, activated her if she was still, made her get to her feet if she was sitting down. It also gave her the power to see beyond the field and the hills and the villages on the plains below to take in the whole country at a glance.

This time they didn't believe her. They knew that exaggeration was the breath of life to her, but they had faith in her ability to see into the unknown, prepare love and hate potions, compose prayers to retrieve lost articles, obtain God's mercy, divert plotters and schemers, make fruit grow bigger, get rid of ants, make a woman beloved by the man she desired, provide a woman with a mirror to reflect the inner thoughts of those who wished her ill, especially a mother-in-law or a co-wife. She even made up special prayers for backbones so that they were not burdened with too many heavy loads. She could make hair grow, stop the stomach demanding more food and, most important of all, compose prayers to awaken passion in husbands so that they came home for a visit, and in bachelors so they thought about marriage. They acknowledged her ability to alter feelings and intentions, for she had been on the verge of reducing. Raifa's husband to a pair of lusting eyes and a male member panting like an asthmatic chest. But Raifa had lost her nerve at the last moment and given the potion, made of a sheet of red ink scribblings soaked in herbs and water, to her nanny goat instead of putting it in her husband's coffee. After that the goat followed Raifa wherever she went, snuffling at the hem of her dress and bleating incessantly to attract her attention. Its excitement reached a peak whenever Raifa bent over or squatted on her haunches as she worked in the field and around the house.

Eventually Raifa lost patience and started running away from the goat or throwing lettuce seeds over it to break the spell, vowing even to put up with her husband. But all her efforts did nothing to curb the goat's lust and in the end her husband, who knew nothing of all this, became convinced that the goat was ill and this was its way of complaining or saying good-bye to its owners. And so one morning he slaughtered it and skinned it and was amazed to see how enlarged its heart was.

However, the women felt sorry for Qut al-Qulub because she was over thirty and not yet married. They knew why she had refused many offers; she and her cousin had been in love, but he had gone and married someone from another village and no longer dared visit Kawkabana.

One day when the women were joking that Qut al-Qulub had missed the boat, she invited them to come and see the dozens of suitors from their village and villages around about who were asking for her hand. The hopeful suitors stood one after another in front of the closed door, which she refused to open. Afterward the women flocked around her, demanding to know why she had rejected them, and she told them that she didn't want a man who was bewitched. "If he embraced me, it would be because I wanted him to. The same if he talked to me or slept beside me. Everything he did would be because I'd decided he should, except going to the bathroom." Then she reconsidered and said, "Even that could be because I wanted him to. Perhaps if I was busy and wanted him out from under my feet for a bit."

Time went by and Qut al-Qulub did not appear to suffer from being unmarried, in fact the opposite. She made it plain that she was happy, saying, "I'm free, comfortably off. I'm Qut al-Qulub, not a beast of burden carrying some man's kids. What's more, marriage stops you feeling feminine and changes the love inside you into children. Your back's killing you from working in the fields and your husband's sitting there calling out, 'Where's my dinner? Where's my qat?' You find you're always trying to snatch a bit of time to go and chat with your friends."

Not content with making comments like these, she would always show her annoyance when she heard of someone getting married or having children: her lip curling with distaste, she would gesture toward her stomach and her breasts and say, "Breast-feeding. All that milk. It's disgusting."

Her hair was parted in the middle, shiny black with not

a trace of gray, not even disguised with henna. She wore coral beads around her neck, and what was astonishing about her was that she was always beautifully adorned. She put kohl around her eyes, one of which was black and one brown. Her headdress was made of material that gleamed like stars and her perfume was a costly essence that she had bought on her travels, mixed with rose water. To make it penetrate the fabric of her clothes thread by thread and never fade, she had constructed a circular stand for her dress out of tree branches and she kept a lighted incense burner under it all night. The other women came to her from daybreak onward and always found her without a hair out of place. When they commented on this, she remarked that she was never alone: if there weren't human beings with her, there were always external forces that she couldn't give a name to. "Jinns?" they asked.

"I don't know," she answered, "but I have conversations with them, so they must be present and able to see me, even if it's only in my mind, so why shouldn't I look as nice as possible for them? Anyway, it makes me stronger and more self-confident."

The moon was full that night. Dogs howled and chased it as it raced from one mountaintop to another. It looked as if you could reach out and touch it, a flat loaf browning in the oven, or half a melon. The custom was that the moment you saw the full moon, you made a secret wish and then kissed the one you were with. So the women kissed one another on the cheeks, saying *basmallas* and making wishes, especially for the crops to ripen in their fields. Then they went on their way in and out of alleyways, under arches, across the open ground between the houses to see Batul, whose husband had been buried exactly a week before. The old women began to hand out advice, telling Batul not to look at the moon because it was male, in case the angels dropped her husband's soul as they headed through the skies toward Paradise. Then as the time passed they all forgot their well-tried sayings and pieces of advice, the widow and her grief slipped their minds and they began unconsciously stealing glances at the moon and the stars, which were nearly coming in through the open window, bringing comfort to their hearts. They were enjoying the view without having to move their bodies, exhausted by the day's work, slumped loosely under their black velvet embroidered dresses with gold and silver belts slung around their hips.

All the women of the village were there except the young girls, who roamed the hills and rooftops as usual, and visited one another's houses, trailed by dogs and younger sisters. Their voices could be heard recriminating, scolding, sometimes laughing, carried by the dry, clear air to the crowd of women in Batul's house.

The gap created by the absence of Qut al-Qulub was

tangible: she was the last bead in the rosary and her presence pulled the other beads together and completed the string. Everything she said aroused the enthusiasm and interest of the others, even though they did not always agree with her. She had been the first to look into the unknown and see oil under the rocks and fields in many different places, and then see Saudi Arabia shaking a finger at foreign oil companies, warning them not to look for oil in Yemen; for it wanted to be the only country with oil so that the Yemenis would not stop working there. She had been right and now the villages were like bags emptied of their contents and thrown to one side, as if war had broken out and all the men had been called up. This was what had happened: the men had abandoned their dark shops, which were no more than wooden cupboards, to go and work in Saudi Arabia, leaving the villages to the women. They visited their families once a year when strings of taxis would arrive from the airport loaded with televisions, videos and blankets. This would go on until they came to the end of their active lives and prepared to face old age and the hereafter by returning home for the last time. They failed to notice that their women had changed completely, even in their way of speaking, and had a special language of their own.

When time passed and still Qut al-Qulub did not join the gathering to offer her condolences to Batul, one of the women went out to the edge of the porch and called her name at the top of her voice. This was the way people normally contacted each other, or had arguments, or announced news, good or bad. But Qut al-Qulub did not appear or call back to explain or apologize. Although the evening passed off satisfactorily without her, they became increasingly anxious. Some of them were more curious than worried and their curiosity was tinged with jealousy. Whatever was stopping her coming must certainly be important, otherwise how could she stay away from an occasion like this? It would become a stain on her past along with the habit she had of going off on trips by herself from time to time, which harmed her reputation, especially as she used to come back tired, absentminded and depressed, then shut herself away and listen to strange music, which she had brought back with her.

The moment they had said good-bye to Batul they hurried off and, as if by an unspoken agreement, went over the rocks and hillocks and along the twisting lanes to the house where Qut al-Qulub lived. There was no light from inside but the outside was lit up by the moon. They shouted at her, reproaching her for not coming, banged on her door, threw little stones at the wooden shutters, but there was no response. They repeated the onslaught once, twice, three times and finally heard her voice asking them to go away because she was working and didn't want to be disturbed, didn't want anything to spoil her concentration. One of them replied derisively, "So you think you're the governor!"

The others laughed for in the next village the children had been obliged to stop playing in their normal rowdy groups at siesta time for a whole month while the provincial governor was visiting his family.

At this Qut al-Qulub opened the window and whispered, "Have you forgotten that there's a full moon above your heads! Leave me alone now and come back tomorrow morning. I promise you, your hair will go white with shock!"

They did not believe her. She must have remembered the gathering at Batul's only after she had removed her headdress. Or perhaps she just had not looked as beautiful as she liked to look. Sometimes she found herself pretty and sometimes really ugly, especially before her period, when she used to say that everything swelled up, even the mole on her cheek, even the little hairs in her eyebrows.

They started shouting again. Laughing, they reminded her of the story of Layla and the monkey shit. They still remembered how some of the magic she had attempted when the moon was full had failed. She had asked Layla to bring her some monkey's feces. Layla's husband had just married another wife, years younger than Layla, and the idea was that when his glance fell on the bewitched feces and then on his new wife, she would seem drab and ugly and give off a smell of shit.

But when he came home and took his new wife in his arms, delighted because she was pregnant less than a month after their marriage, Layla was sure he hadn't even noticed the stuff. She tried putting it somewhere more conspicuous and her husband simply remarked that it was the feces of an animal not found in the village. She conveyed this information to Qut al-Qulub, who would not believe that she had failed but would only concede that the shit must have been bogus. In any case, how could Layla have procured it, when a snowfall was just about as likely as a monkey in this village! She didn't believe that Layla had hitched a ride with a medical mission that had passed through the village one day and gone to Taiz, where there was a cage full of monkeys by the museum gateway. She accused her of lying and when bystanders intervened to confirm that Layla was telling the truth she said they were hypocrites. A few days later Layla returned accompanied by a procession of children, old people and youths, all eager to tell Qut al-Qulub about the monkey Layla had bought with the proceeds from her gold jewelry. Qut al-Qulub came to examine the monkey and was delighted. She had never seen one before. Its small, searching eyes pleased her and she muttered that at last she understood the secret of the magic hidden in its eyes. Those who heard what she said were afraid that she might demand its eyes for her witchcraft, but she asked to be left alone with it, then came out and told Layla that the shit had to be black. But Layla's husband took his second wife in his arms again, curious to know the identity of the strange beast that had emptied its bowels in front of his house, in case its flesh was good to eat. Qut al-Qulub claimed again that the shit was not black enough and the whole village went on trying to think of some food that would make it really black, without much success. Eventually the story leaked out through the women and children, Layla's husband came to hear of it and went crazy because his wife had spent so much money and sold her jewelry for the sake of some monkey shit. He swore he would take a third wife and so he did.

The women started shouting again, calling to Qut al-Qulub to show herself. In the end her scowling face appeared at the window. She warned them to keep away from her house and respect what she was trying to achieve on this momentous night, promising that she would show them the results in the morning.

With one accord, they retreated a few steps in silence, then returned as if bewitched to their places in front of the house. The moon was shining directly above it. They were happy with the night, despite their grief over the dead man and his widow. Their visit to Batul had actually made them content and grateful and they praised the Lord that their husbands were still in the land of the living, not in the next world like Batul's, especially since he'd died in Saudi Arabia and she'd had to pay for the transportation of the body and its burial here in the village. What's more, his wages had stopped and from now on she'd have to rely solely on what she grew in the field. This death in the village reminded them how lucky they were, brought it home to them that they were married yet free.

So wide were their eyes with sleeplessness that they seemed to fill the whole of their faces. The women appeared confused, circling around the house, sitting down, standing up. They were convinced that vibrations given off by Qut al-Qulub had drawn them here, with the intervention of the moon. It was said that people had walked on the moon. At the time the village sheikh had broadcast from the minaret that a cow must be slaughtered to atone for the moon's defilement.

They would have remained under the sway of Qut al-Qulub and their own euphoria had they not heard the voice of the billy goat. "We've even woken the goat," remarked Raifa. Then she sang a song that came into her head at that moment:

Come my love and see
I've bought you some qat

Feed it to that little bird
And he'll become a billy goat with horns

When they turned instinctively to look at Qut al-Qulub's goat as if awaiting its reaction to Raifa's song, they found that it was not in its usual spot.

They went all around the outside of the house looking for it, convinced that Qut al-Qulub had forgotten to tie it up and that it was wandering alone in the mountains. They were a little worried about it but their concern led to much hilarity as Raifa imitated the goat leaping high in the air when the dogs nipped its hindquarters, which was what happened to Wajiha's donkey. Raifa started calling to Qut al-Qulub, telling her that her goat had escaped and was lost, but instead of Qut al-Qulub answering, the goat bleated, and the sound came from inside the house. At this the women's confusion mounted, clouding their vision. It was this confusion that led Raifa to call out once, twice, three times asking Qut al-Qulub about the goat, until at last they heard her voice shout back insolently, "Now do you believe me? The goat's with me. That should prove to you that I'm absorbed in my work."

They went back to their homes and the sound of their snoring rose in the air as soon as they threw themselves onto cushions in their living rooms, too tired even to put down their mattresses. The next day they brought the bread to the oven to bake as they did every morning, milked the sheep, collected the eggs, then prepared coffee with ginger before hurrying off to the field in the valley, where they grew walnuts, qat, wheat, fenugreek and vegetables. When they met Qut al-Qulub at the pond with her goat drinking at her side, they asked her where she had found it, flatly refusing to acknowledge her claims of the previous night. As if she understood, she too acted as if nothing had happened and contented herself with patting the goat's neck, stroking its horns, brushing some specks of mud off its coat and waving a fly away from its eyes. Ignoring this pantomime, they continued with their efforts to find her out, and asked her why she had not turned up to visit Batul. She answered them with a huge ringing laugh, throwing her head back so that all her teeth and her uvula were on show. Then she began to tell them about the silver light of the moon, but the women did not listen. They walked away from her in exasperation and went to work in the field. It was as if the subject of Qut al-Qulub no longer had any significance since the events of the night before. They put all their efforts into their toil under the burning sun, singing together or letting one woman sing alone to break up the day's monotony, amusing themselves by talking to the animals that helped them with harvesting and carrying, studying the position of the sun and clouds, examining one another's crops and muttering *basmallas* to ward off the evil eye.

That night Qut al-Qulub's goat disappeared again and she shut herself away as she had done before. This might have been forgotten within a few days if the goat had not appeared the next morning streaked with henna. Layla examined it and informed the other women that it had a different look in its eyes from before. The women did not inquire further or comment on the goat's transformation. Instead they increased the number of *basmallas* they said when they found themselves face-to-face with Qut al-Qulub or caught her looking in their direction. They had instructed their children from an early age to say "God protect us" to themselves whenever she came in sight.

When the goat disappeared and Qut al-Qulub shut herself away for the third night in a row, Layla and Raifa hurried to her house. They had been delegated by the others to go alone, as it would have made too much noise if they had all gone. They searched for any traces of the goat, keeping their movements restrained so that not even a small exhalation of breath escaped their lips. They clung unblinking to the wall hour after hour until they heard the goat making a commotion inside the house as if it was kicking its hooves against something. Minutes went by. Nothing but silence and waiting. Raifa looked at Layla as if she hoped she too was having second thoughts about being there. When Layla did not respond, Raifa motioned with her head that they should leave. Layla moved her head slowly from side to side in a gesture of refusal, then looked in front of her, making her eyes soft as if begging her companion to be patient. Silence. Silence. Silence and then the sound of a throat being cleared in the still air, deafening them and making their hearts stop beating. It was not Qut al-Qulub or any other woman, nor the goat or any other animal. Was it a spirit? Then there was Qut al-Qulub saying, "Bless you."

The two women shook their heads in horror. Qut al-Qulub would never talk to a spirit in such a homely way, as if she was sitting beside it. Confusion, fantasy, conjecture and logic mingled wildly in their heads, and without saying anything they slipped away back to the others to receive confirmation and reassurance that they were still sane, for they were picturing the strangest scenes. The other women believed them without much hesitation. The two of them had become like bats using sound vibrations to construct a detailed image of their prey and its whereabouts.

They pictured that Qut al-Qulub had changed the man she loved into a goat—for she had sworn when news of his marriage reached her that she would have her revenge on him even if it took years. They also pictured that she had managed to change the goat into a man who was a replica of her beloved. Then they reverted to the first version and decided that, having bewitched him, she had forgiven him and turned him back into a man, or that she had tried before and had succeeded only in the past three days, or that she was still in the process of bewitching him. Was the village not already familiar with the story of the magician who used to turn her lover into a donkey in the day and back into a man at night, all to avoid the talk and the violence of the men in her family, since her lover was from another tribe?

There was no other explanation, for even though the two women had been certain that it was a man they heard coughing, there was nowhere in the village she could have found one. In the graveyard? In the photographs in pride of place on living room walls? In the worn clothes left hanging on a nail because the men had to be dressed in their best when they went away to work? In their voices sent to their families on cassettes because they didn't know how to write and their women didn't know how to read? There was no trace of them there except in memories, and can a memory give birth to a man of flesh and bone?

So the two women slipped away from Qut al-Qulub's house like hairs from flour and gradually fear began to take hold of them, despite their curiosity and the shock of discovery, and they repeated *basmallas* and recited the prayer to drive away fear, only to ask God's forgiveness again for it was a prayer composed by Qut al-Qulub.

The village rapidly became like a watermelon being tapped to find out if it was red and sweet-tasting inside.

Layla's daughter was the only one to remind them that Qut al-Qulub had tried to explain what was really going on when they asked about the goat. As soon as she began talking about the silver moon and the way it worked miracles for her, they had walked off. The women listened to Layla's daughter for a moment, then went back to their noisy debate. They wished there were just one man in the village, somebody's husband or brother, whom they could consult. They had wished this often before, when one of the children or animals became ill, or the traps they set for the birds that ate the seeds failed to work. Then they said they wished their village was close to the other villages, instead of being up in the clouds, so they could seek help from a man of religion. The fact that the mosque had no Quran reciter and no muezzin must mean that there was a way for magic to interfere with religious belief. Then once more they blamed the location of their village—the influence of the moonlight must be twice as strong as in other villages.

They thought again about hiding from the moon, out of range of its bright beams, but quickly put the thought out of their minds, not wanting to hasten an eclipse and bring bad luck on themselves. All these fantasies were little more than ways of dulling the persistent notion that they must see what was really going on in Qut al-Qulub's house.

So moving forward like a column of black ants, their black shawls covering their heads, their black dresses raised so they would not impede their progress and the henna on their dry feet hardly touching the ground, they passed through the main gate in the wall and on through the other entrances so they could go to her on the rocky track beyond the village. Then if the dogs howled and Qut al-Qulub looked out, she would see no trace of them. They went by the pond and the moonlight made the green moss on the water's surface look like strange insects. Then they encircled Qut al-Qulub's house, which fitted into the circumference of the mountain like a silkworm wrapping itself around a mulberry leaf. The dark windows surrounded by white plaster looked like watching eyes.

The sight of the closed door and the high windows discouraged them, but then a light shone suddenly in a window, their eyes fell on the goat's empty patch and they felt a renewed surge of curiosity about what was taking place in the house.

Each woman had a different image of what she was going to see inside: a goatskin lying on the floor and the man whom Qut al-Qulub had loved standing there as large as life, imploring her to turn him back into a man for good, kissing her feet contritely; a man's head on a goat's body or the other way around; a goat begging her not to turn it back into a human being because it did not like dealing with humankind: "I've had enough of their evil ways. Especially yours."

Their curiosity rose to delirium, increasing their strength and eagerness, and they formed a pyramid, each on another's shoulders, until Raifa reached the window and saw the lamp lighting up the room. But it was really the moon that illuminated the room, making it as bright as day, so that Raifa could see Qut al-Qulub lying on her side, smoking a cigarette, her hair spread out around her. Most of her flesh was exposed and beside her was the man who had brought back the body of Batul's husband.

The Holiday

The following is an essay I wrote describing a day in my school holidays.

That day was different from the rest of the spring holidays. The rain came down in torrents, the grass was sodden and my grandmother stood at the window examining the sky, waiting for the clouds to break and a patch of blue to appear. When this didn't happen she took off her black coat and went back to bed as she nearly always did when it rained. I opened my mouth and started to cry, only stopping when my father said impatiently, "Come with me, then!"

My mother tried to step in but I was too quick for them. I sat in my father's car, chanting, "My dad loves me. We're going for a drive, and he's going to buy me lots of things."

But as he drove along, cursing the traffic and the hole in his exhaust, aiming straight at the puddles, ignoring the people on foot, the picture I had in my mind of him taking me shopping disappeared fast, although I continued my song until he stopped the car suddenly at a row of food shops.

"Don't you dare move. Be still as a statue," he instructed as he left me.

I wound down the window and stuck my head out, looking at the things on display and wondering why each shopper bought something different. When I was sick of watching the people, I started to observe the drops of rain and decided that they had no idea in advance where they were going to fall. A traffic policeman stood staring at the car but didn't come up to it until my father reappeared holding a plastic carrier bag that contained a freshly slaughtered chicken with blood still drying stiffly around its head.

The policeman nodded his head knowingly as he told

my father off for displaying his doctor's permit and parking where he wasn't meant to. My father fished his card out of his pocket and answered, "Twenty-four-hour service. If you need a checkup, any pills, just call me."

He tore off along the side streets, ignoring my song, then crossed a little bridge and plunged down a steep road, making my heart miss a beat, before he stopped finally and said, "Here we are, Layla. Now the nurse'll give you a sweet."

We'd only gone a short distance from the car when my father remembered his white coat and went back, holding me firmly by the hand. He let go of me while he unlocked the car and rummaged around among old newspapers and plastic containers for urine samples and different kinds of medicine until he found his white doctor's coat at last. We entered a building that didn't even smell like a hospital. My father went up to a man sitting at a table in the corridor and introduced himself with pride. "I'm the new public health inspector. Here and in the red light district. Every brothel in town."

I hadn't heard the word *brothel* before, but I felt pleased that my father was a public health inspector, and then ashamed all at once when he put on his white coat and I saw that it was covered in stains. We went into one of the rooms off the corridor and a nun came rushing after us.

"Where are you going?" she asked my father, with a disapproving look in my direction.

He repeated what he'd said to the man sitting at the table, and she seemed satisfied and greeted him, and then turned to me and asked me if I was still on my school holidays. And she took out a brightly colored boiled sweet from the pocket of her white habit.

The room was cold, and empty except for some iron bedsteads without proper bedding on them, and a little girl with gold teeth who was washing the floor and looking in my direction. My father spoke to her bossily. "Wash it nicely. There's a clever girl."

Then he opened his bag and took out some medicine, which he pressed into the nun's hand. "Here are some vitamins for her. She's such a skinny little thing. These'll make her stronger. Put a bit of flesh on her legs!"

Then he began talking to the beds: "Come on! Up you get! This isn't a hotel."

The faded blankets stirred and several women's faces emerged from them, opening their eyes blankly, reminding me at once of the chicken in the plastic carrier. I stared at them, fascinated by their sickly color, which matched the blankets. I supposed the women must be very ill, because they looked like Hassan's mother, who used to be lying in bed whenever I went to play with Hassan. He was proud of having the only mother with a face that color, but in the end she died from being so pale. When the women in the beds closed their eyes again I stood fidgeting, feeling bored, then I heard the nun saying in an Armenian accent, "There were five of them, Doctor. One escaped."

For a moment my father didn't speak, just nodded his head, but then he said, "Where did she think she was going? They'll pick her up again straightaway."

He bent over his bag and selected an instrument like the tongue of a shoe. I had often seen it before and played with it sometimes when I found it lying around. He seemed to be holding a conversation with it as he wiped it on his dirty white coat: "Let's have a look. Slip your pants off."

I stood rooted to the spot in disbelief. "Have you been examined before, or are you new to the job?" he went on, still wiping the instrument. I didn't know who he was talking to as none of the women moved. Then one turned her face away and looked as if she were trying to burrow into the wall.

The nun went over to the first bed and ordered its occupant to hurry up because the doctor was very busy. The woman shifted in the bed but her lifeless eyes never changed, as if her head were not connected to her body. My father marched up and pulled the cover aside like he did when I was hiding down in the bed. The woman tried to arrange herself, tugging her nightdress down over her thighs, but my father was shouting at her: "So you're acting like the Virgin Mary now! You should have done that yesterday when they caught you with your heels in the air!"

Then he turned to the nun and asked her where they'd been rounded up. "The cemetery at Sinn Al-Fil," she answered disapprovingly.

My father swung around to the women again, telling them in that same loud, harsh voice that they must be stupid if they preferred graveyards to the red light district, whose advantages he then listed for them: apart from regular examinations by him, there were clean, tidy rooms with hot running water, and as if that weren't enough they had the best baker in town just across the street.

My father hitched the woman's nightdress up so high that I could see her large stomach. The lower part of it wasn't like mine, but more like my mother's, covered with little hairs. He moved in on her with a spyglass; the woman brought her legs together and he forced them roughly apart, then asked the nun to have a look. But the nun turned away in disgust and so did I. My father bent closer as if he couldn't believe his eyes. He told her she was a filthy cow and warned her that she'd die if she didn't do as he said and take the medicines he prescribed. Then he moved on to the next one and got ready to examine her, when his eyes fell on the last bed. Maybe he was calculating how many more examinations he had to do, and suddenly the tiny red veins in his nose looked as if they were about to explode. He called out a name, "Nafisa," and swore and spluttered as if he didn't know what to say.

He rushed over to the last bed and pulled the blanket away from the woman's pretty face, accusing her of turning her back on everything good, telling her she had no conscience, nothing, only what she carried between her legs and hawked around the streets. Then he stopped and looked about him and remembered that I was still there. He said soothingly that we were going on the best outing ever, and took my hand, turning to the nun: "I'm going to get her husband."

Letting my hand drop he returned to Nafisa's bedside and shook her furiously by the shoulders, shouting, "How could you? Men are your protection. Why didn't you stay with him? You've had it now. Your brother'll get to hear about this in no time, and then you'll be sorry!"

He took hold of my hand again and hurried to the door, closely pursued by the nun, who was trying desperately to persuade him to finish examining the other women. He assured her that he'd be back but he had to find Nafisa's husband before he vanished too.

We were almost gone when Nafisa's voice stopped us. "Can I have a word, Doctor?"

"To hell with you! I know exactly what you're going to say." He mimicked her voice. "Never again, Doctor. I'll never do it again."

"Doctor! If only he had just given me a roof over my head and forgotten about my past! Everything I do and say is an excuse for him to bring it up. He threatens to send me back where he got me. If I wear lipstick he goes crazy. 'So you miss whoring?' he says. When I went to visit his sister in hospital, he thought I'd gone back on the game and went and checked with her and she swore I'd been there. He still didn't believe it, though, and dragged me all around the other patients in the ward. Some of them could scarcely breathe, but it didn't stop him from asking them if they'd seen me visiting his sister."

My father muttered, "God help us," and nothing more, but I sensed that he was no longer so angry with her. She burst into a fit of sobbing and said jerkily between the sniffing and gulping, "He was convinced I was lying. So I said to myself, 'Right, girl! You might as well go back and earn a pound or two.' "

We went off in the car again and I didn't risk asking my father any questions. He was driving fast and lighting a cigarette, forgetting that he had one lit already. He sighed and muttered to himself, cursing because we were going to be late and the chicken would no longer be fresh.

"What did Nafisa do that made you so cross?" I demanded at last.

Instead of answering me, he turned off at a steep slope. That was the end of my last feeble hope that we might be going past the shops for him to buy me something, but I didn't care.

He stopped the car and told me to follow him. We made our way along a muddy path across the grass. I couldn't help stepping in the puddles even though he kept warning me not to. The cars on the road below looked tiny and far away. I wasn't used to being so high up and my heart sank in terror at the thought of slipping and rolling all the way down onto the road. I clutched my father's hand tightly.

The path took us right to the top of the hill, where there was a broad, open space like a fairground at holiday time, but it was full of sheep instead of children. They were everywhere and I wanted to rush up and stroke their wool and sing, "Little lamb, little lamb, how beautiful you are!"

But when we got nearer, I changed my mind and stood motionless, as never before had I seen sheep in such numbers and at such close quarters. Their wool was mud stained, with shreds of old newspaper and garbage clinging to it. They called out like small children as if they were in pain or had lost their mothers, not like in the picture in the reading book, where they are happily grazing. Perhaps the thin, straggly grass wasn't enough for them and they were crying out in hunger. Their owners were strange-looking men, unlike anyone I'd seen before: short, with scowling faces and gold teeth flashing through the smoke that came in puffs out of their mouths when they spoke, even though I couldn't see any cigarettes. They wore high black boots and black fur hats.

My father began asking for Amin from Aleppo, Amin the sheep trader, leading me from one noisy group of men to another, sometimes cutting straight through the middle of the flocks of sheep and other times skirting around them. Finally he stopped in front of a thick-set man. When this man noticed my father he muttered, "Hallo, Doctor," in a very cold voice.

My father immediately kissed him on both cheeks and whispered something in his ear. The man stepped backward but my father took hold of him by the shoulders and tried to talk to him again. Amin's lambs bleated at the tops of their voices. He moved back, trying to escape my father's words. Then he stuck his little finger in his ear, scratched vigorously, examined the piece of yellow wax on his long fingernail for some time and wiped it off on his jacket. At last he spoke, loudly so that he could be heard over his flock. "What I ought to do is take her to the slaughterhouse and cut her throat." He jabbed a finger in the direction of a building I hadn't noticed before. "I'd be well within my rights."

Cut Nafisa's throat? I couldn't take in what he was saying and didn't dare ask either of them to explain.

I was quite sure that silence was necessary on this occasion and, rather than fidgeting impatiently as I normally do when grown-ups talk together and leave me with nothing to do, I stood absolutely still, eager to catch each word.

"Take it easy," advised my father.

"What do you think I've been doing?" the man burst out viciously. "If I hadn't made myself calm down, she'd be dead by now. Believe me, when I heard they'd caught her I grabbed a knife and started out to look for her. I was out of my mind."

So people could be slaughtered just like chickens and sheep. Was that possible? I looked over to the slaughter-house, filled with fear and confusion. They couldn't kill Nafisa. I watched men carrying dozens of fleeces and sheep carcasses slung over their shoulders and loading them onto a lorry, and convinced myself Nafisa wasn't going to have her throat cut, because I couldn't imagine her dangling down a porter's back like that. I heaved a sigh of relief as I saw my father hand the man a cigarette and reach out to light it for him.

The man clapped my father on the shoulder and I stared at the outer wall of the slaughterhouse. It was stained with the reddish-purple color that we learned the Phoenicians had discovered in snail shells. The bleating grew louder as a new lot of sheep was driven toward the building. They must have known that this building was the afterlife, the hell which the teacher is always telling us about.

Their cries grew louder and I pitied them and found myself reaching out to touch a woolly tail. "Little lamb, little lamb, how beautiful you are!" I chanted under my breath. It turned to look at me. Had it heard me? I smiled but its eyes were unseeing like glass.

Do You Know Someone Who Can Teach Me the Piano?

My mother always threatened me when we had a visitor. She wagged her finger at me if I refused to follow her into the kitchen to receive her threats face-to-face, and gave me a look that I understood meant I wasn't to talk too much. If I ignored her and sat down comfortably with one leg crossed over the other, giving my opinion on everything that was discussed, talking rashly about subjects I didn't understand, my father would come quietly across to me and put a big towel over my knees. I heard him saying, "Azrael," under his breath: I knew this was the name of the Angel of Death, but I didn't know if he was scolding me or praying for me to be spared.

My father was a devout man and the sight of my bare knees pained him. He had tried without success to make me cover my head and arms, then channeled his piety toward my legs.

When he covered me up with a towel, he didn't know that he was also gagging me and reducing me to silence. I would freeze, wishing the ground would swallow me up, and soon slink away to my room.

He was only pious about physical things. Otherwise he was broad-minded and allowed me to talk and joke with my brother's friends. He was pleased to see me borrowing books from young male neighbors, and when he heard me arguing a point he would announce to the assembled company that he was going to put me through law school. My brother used to ask him what was wrong with dressmaking, and he would smile kindly, not realizing my brother was joking, and say, "Shame on you! She's the most intelligent girl in the world!"

Although my brother moved north to teach in a government school, his friends continued to visit and stay overnight, as some of them lived down south. For some reason, in the presence of these youths I felt like a toy with a new battery. I paraded my knowledge on any subject, talked at length about Jurji Zaydan's stories and the Rock Hudson film *Never Say Goodbye,* introducing a few English words into my conversation, which I mispronounced. I made them laugh with my impersonations of movie actors. My talk was peppered with lies and exaggerations. Whenever I sensed that my openness was making them awkward, I plunged on without a pause, even using my new surge of power to hide my embarrassment sometimes.

I was twelve when the piano became my obsession. Nobody escaped my question: "Do you know anyone who plays the piano?"

I didn't ask them if they could play themselves, as I knew the answer in advance. I kept repeating untruthfully that the music teacher had told me that a brilliant future awaited me if I learned the piano.

Among those to whom I put my by now habitual question was a boy from the south called Khalil, who stayed with us when he came to Beirut to collect his monthly salary. He was so shy and taciturn that I used to wonder how he explained the lessons to his pupils, and if he ever cracked a joke in class or shouted at them. When we talked to him, he lowered his head and didn't reply and when my parents asked him a direct question, he would answer with his eyes fastened on the toes of his shoes. I don't remember him ever talking to me before that day, still less answering one of my questions.

My mother used to make up a bed for him on the sitting room floor after supper. As soon as everybody was in bed, and the rooms were dark and silent, he switched on the radio and listened to it until late into the night. This annoyed my mother so much that she considered asking him to pay half the electricity bill. Although I knew how shy and awkward he was, I asked him the question that preoccupied me more than any other. I was sure he didn't know anyone who played the piano, but when he ignored me I asked him again, and he merely raised his eyes from the floor in response. For the first time I noticed his long black eyelashes and wondered how he could be so timid when he had such beautiful eyes. The third time, to my surprise, he answered me, or asked me a question in return: "Why do you think I'd know someone who plays the piano?"

His answer-question disconcerted me. "I just thought you would," I said lamely.

My inhibitions didn't last, and the next time he came, as I was setting out the dishes of *zaatar*—thyme and olive oil—and cream cheese and olives for his breakfast, I asked again. He looked away from me. He began staring hard at the piece of bread he'd taken and crumbling it in his fingers. Before I could press him further, my mother called me in a voice that broke the sound barrier. Although I was standing before her in no time, she didn't lower the volume. "To hell with you and your piano," she shouted. "You're driving us all crazy. Stop pestering that poor boy. I hope they put a piano on your grave so that you can strum it in eternity till you're sick of it."

It didn't often bother me when my mother shouted at me, but this time was different. Khalil must have heard. With her shouting, my brightly colored hula-hoop socks, my jingling bangles, the English words I knew, all evaporated into nothing. I stood paralyzed outside the door of the living room, with an empty tray in my hand. My mother gave me a push and told me to hurry up and get the plates off the table, or else. I found myself in the middle of the room, desperately hoping that he wouldn't have heard. But he had, because he cleared his throat self-consciously. I didn't look at him. I couldn't even breathe. I went discreetly up to the table, and to my amazement I heard him say consolingly, "I've got a friend who studies music at the Conservatoire. I'll try and bring him with me next time I come."

I turned to look at him and found him with his head bowed as usual: it was as if someone else had spoken the words, or they had descended as a revelation from heaven. On this occasion I hid my embarrassment and confusion by putting on a smile and saying with a squeal of delight, "How nice of you! Make sure you don't forget!"

A month passed, and Khalil didn't come to stay with us as usual. My mother thought she must have offended him when she asked him for ten pounds because he bumped into the radio one night and knocked it onto the floor. Meanwhile I was convinced that he was avoiding me because he didn't really know anyone who could teach me the piano.

I no longer counted the days to the end of the month. I started asking everyone who visited us my usual question again, until I heard that Khalil had been found one morning hanging from the rafters in the school where he taught in the south.

The Keeper of the Virgins

One of the women wondered aloud if he was a dwarf in every way. The other women sitting at the intersection burst out laughing. Even though they prayed to God to forgive them, their laughter grew louder before the dwarf was out of sight.

They had grown used to seeing him every morning shortly after they set to work, bending over the hibiscus bushes to gather the wine-colored blossoms. He would go by with a confident step, heading for the convent, where the pure ones lived, books and magazines tucked under his arm, a cloth bundle containing his food for the day held firmly in his hand. He was content to greet the hibiscus pickers as he passed, although they welcomed him enthusiastically and offered him a glass of tea or some warm bread. He knew it was because he was a dwarf and they felt sorry for him, but he had a great sense of his own importance. Besides keeping up with the politics of his own country and the Arab world in general, he had broadened his interests to take in the whole planet. He studied thoroughly and remembered everything he learned, delved into dictionaries, read novels, both translated and local, and underlined passages in pencil when the subject matter appealed to him or he liked the sound of the words. He wrote poetry and prose, and sent it to newspapers and magazines, even though not a single line of it had ever been published; and he had been going to the convent and waiting by the main gates in its outer wall for a year or more.

He would sit in the generous shade of a sycamore tree or lie on a blanket he had brought with him beneath its spreading branches, staring at the convent walls. He had learned the shape of their dusty red stones by heart; their uneven surfaces and the way they were arranged reminded him of a tray of the vermicelli pastries called *kunafa.* He spent these long stretches of time either reading, sometimes to himself and sometimes out loud, or building a fire with a few sticks to make tea, or waiting for the hoopoe, which appeared out of nowhere from the direction of the trees and the water or from the bare, stony desert. Every now and then he would stare hard at the iron gates of the convent, hearing some kind of a commotion on the other side. But he was convinced that it was a figment of his imagination because the place was always calm and still again at once, as if there had been no interruption.

But as the days went by he discovered from one of the men building the nearby tombs, who sat and chatted with him for a while each evening, that the noise he heard was real enough, as the nuns used to sweep the convent yard every now and then. This ruined his concentration for some considerable length of time: he could not read with such enthusiasm, or savor a choice sentence or the hot sweetness of a glass of tea or the food he brought with him. He became entirely focused on the iron gates, as if by staring at them he could melt them and make them collapse before his eyes.

During his first few weeks of frequenting the monastery, he had tried to have a conversation with the nuns to persuade them to open the gate, but each time his request had been refused in dumb silence. He had asked if he could sweep the yard for nothing, worship in the church, confess, but still he met with no response from behind the closed gates. Gradually he became convinced that everybody had joined forces to concoct a lie about the existence of this convent, because he was a dwarf, and he knew very well what people thought about dwarves. They were all lying to him: the tomb builders, the hibiscus women, his family, the wind, which must have cooperated with them by making some noise behind the abandoned gates; Georgette's mother, who had lamented long and loud because her daughter had joined the pure ones and their door had closed behind her, never to open again.

Georgette's family must be hiding the truth. Georgette must have gone mad and been locked away, for just before the rumor went around that she had entered the convent, she would only leave the house to walk over thorns until her feet bled.

The dwarf became convinced that many people profited from his visits to the convent. His mother regularly rose at dawn to get his food ready, as if he had a job to go to. His younger brother must have heaved a sigh of relief at this new routine of his, for however much he might love the dwarf, he had to be forced to let him participate in his nights out with his friends. They all used to sit in the dwarf's presence as if they were on eggs, wary of any joke or chance phrase that might offend him or hurt his feelings. Still, he couldn't remember his brother ever praising him for his determination when he saw him preparing to go to the convent, nor even the hibiscus women, who must have relished the chance to invent hilarious, irreverent stories about him. And what did the tomb builders think of him? He couldn't bear to let these thoughts torment him anymore, and hurried resolutely to bang on the gates with his giant hands. As usual, he asked for Georgette. He wanted to see her, to thank her for the affection she had heaped on him. Time stood still and he felt as if all the power in his body was in his huge, solid fist with its wide-apart fingers. As he was about to start hammering on the gates again, he heard a soft voice whispering to him that Georgette said hello but seeing her was out of the question.

From that moment on he began to have a fixation about the convent. The iron gates, bolted and barred, had an obsessive hold over him. Georgette's mother had wailed that she would never see her daughter again even when she died. How did they exist in there for all those years without being tempted to step over the threshold for a moment?

The gates, unmoved by his devotion to them, had opened a few times when he was not there; he had discovered their treachery by looking for evidence each morning, and had found tire tracks made by cars, trucks and mule-drawn carts. He brought his face close to the ground to find out whether the gates had been opened wide or only on one side, biting his lip in remorse because he had missed a chance to see the pure ones as they opened the gates and took the things and paid for them. Where did they get the money from?

As time passed, the dwarf grew ever more obsessed with the convent and its inhabitants. He no longer tried to explain it, and those who saw him waiting regularly at the gates ceased to worry about him. No doubt they told themselves that it was something to do with the way dwarves looked at things, and their different mentality.

Then one night the dwarf failed to return home. His mother wept loudly, blaming herself for not stopping his visits to the convent before. She was sure that a wild animal had blocked his path and eaten him in one mouthful. His brother suspected that a group of acrobats had kidnapped him and taken him to the city to train him to work in the circus.

He set off for the convent at high speed. He passed the hibiscus gatherers and they directed him to it. One of them winked at him, so he thought better of asking if they had seen the dwarf. The moment he stood before the gates he was seized by a violent sense of apprehension. One last grain of hope had remained, but there was no sign of the dwarf, only the tree and the blanket that he had hung over a branch and the stone where he used to sit; a few empty soap-powder cartons, which had been blown up against the walls; and crushed and broken coffins, some lined with black material and emblazoned with white crosses. The wind whistled and in the distance he could see the builders at work on new tombs. He shouted his brother's name and was answered by silence. He began to blame himself. He had known that his brother was running away from reality by taking refuge at the convent, making everyone think that he was strong enough to do the daily round-trip on foot, about four hours in all, so that he could come home proud of having had some adventures.

Adventures? The roads were always the same: deserted, except for stretches of date palms, canals and the sounds of frogs croaking and an occasional donkey braying.

The brother stumbled hurriedly over the remains of human bones and crumbling skulls and entered a burial chamber with no roof or doors. He read on its whitewashed walls, "Remember, O Lord, your obedient servant"; "Remember, O Lord, your erring servant"; "Remember, O Lord, your righteous servant, your repentant servant." Suddenly he burst into tears, mortified that deep down inside he had blessed his brother's daily visits to the convent. He had not wanted it to be known that he was the dwarf's brother, that he lived under the same roof as the dwarf. He rushed outside and over to the tomb builders. One of them was painting a tomb a reddish-brown color and he asked him if he had seen the dwarf. The man pointed toward the convent. He turned and ran back and pounded on the iron gates, calling out the dwarf's name. To his astonishment he heard his voice: "Yes?"

"Thank God you're safe," he said, crying tears of joy. "Come on, let's go home, or your mother will do herself mischief."

"Don't worry," replied the dwarf. "Tell her that I've become the nuns' watchman. I'm happy. Don't worry."

The dwarf had only gained access to the convent by jumping in. Not by bouncing in off a springy bedstead, an idea he had quickly banished from his mind, nor by piling the wrecked coffins one on top of another. Instead he had jumped onto the shoulders of the Lord Bishop, who had come from the city to pay his annual visit to the convent with several crates of luggage. The dwarf had planned for this moment for a long time during his vigils by the gate. He didn't know where he had found the courage, agility and speed of thought that had enabled him to leap out as soon as he heard the car engine and alight on the hood before it stopped, like a winged insect, then jump on the Lord Bishop and relieve him of one of the crates and rush off with it, his heart beating with almost unbearable ferocity. He hurried disbelievingly through the open gates into the courtyard. To force himself to take in what was happening, he stood stock-still at the gates once they had been closed again, seeing them from the inside for the first time. He was certain that they would be opened again shortly and he would be hurled back outside. But things no longer hinged on him. It was as if he had disappeared from sight. The nuns began to gather around in their white habits and crowns of artificial flowers, bowing their heads before the Lord Bishop, who looked like a big black bird, and bending over to kiss his hand.

They were like brides, some of them extremely young and pretty. As they stood in line, their heads drooping bashfully, they resembled a row of beautiful narcissus. For a few moments the dwarf felt embarrassed and scared. He tried to suppress his breathing, which had suddenly become audible. Then he found the Lord Bishop was looking at him. "Is this the one?" he was asking.

One of them, the senior nun, answered him humbly, but with affection, "Yes, My Lord."

Turning back to him the bishop said, "The nuns have told me about you. You have been blessed. You will watch over them."

The dwarf felt awkward in the bishop's presence. He didn't know how to answer him. He had been immensely curious to see what was behind the gates; it was like the time he split a battery in two to see what was inside it. And now the bishop was offering him a job as a handyman to the pure ones, and he found himself agreeing to stay in the convent and oversee the cultivation of the fruit and vegetables, without giving the matter more than a moment's thought.

He hadn't imagined the convent would be like this. It bore no relation to its outer walls and to the countryside around it, which was all sand, and the color of sand. The dwarf developed an attachment to the colors in the convent in his early days there. Some of them he was seeing for the first time, sculpted on the walls, or in paintings of animals, bats, angels, flowers, and women holding drums and wearing ornate brocade dresses, flying through the skies or in boats on the sea, with lances and daggers and swords in the background. Then gradually his eyes grew accustomed to the darkness, and he began to see clearly and especially to notice how the nuns lit up the place in their white clothes.

A week went by and the dwarf still hadn't guessed which was Georgette, because they all looked the same. Humbly, they took turns to kneel and pray before the statue of the crucified Christ until their eyes were almost as big as goose eggs. They didn't leave the statue alone day or night, massaging its feet with rose water, putting compresses soaked with oil and perfume on the nails of the crucifix, lighting candles, burning incense, and raising their voices in sweet, sorrowful chanting. They dedicated themselves to their love so wholeheartedly that he once had the feeling that all they did was hover in the air awaiting their turn to cling to the figure on the cross for a few moments before going back to their places. He didn't know why, on a certain day, they brought in a doll and dipped it in water, praying all the time, then rubbed it with colored stones that gave off an enticing fragrance, dried it with an embroidered cloth and dressed it in white baby clothes, which they had taken from a cloth bag studded with precious stones and tied with ropes of pearls.

They were eaten up heart and soul with their love for Christ. This was true love, the like of which he had never found in any novel, translated or otherwise. Never before had he encountered such passion and devotion. Was this what they called sacrifice? The dwarf checked himself. Of course. They had sacrificed the world and their families for the sake of this love, or for the sake of competing for this love. Closing his eyes, he decided to respond to their love, to help them realize that Christ knew about them and the way they showed their love for him. Moreover, Christ had sent the dwarf as a messenger to them. Wasn't that what the old nun had said? He would help those who were waiting their turn to love Christ by doing their embroidery with them, or by changing the linen in the church. He would snatch the washing out of the boiling water to save them from having to do it. He would have liked to hang it up to dry in the scorching sun, but he wasn't tall enough to reach the washing line. He would light the coals and fan them until they were glowing embers and load them into the flat-iron. He would plant flowers and pick them for the garlands they wore on their heads, so that they didn't have to use artificial flowers. He would feed the hens with grain day and night until they were bursting with health and well-being and laid the choicest eggs in the country. He'd polish the nuns' shoes until they could see their faces in them. He'd make their mud-brick beds for them and be close to their sheets—for Christ must smell that they were clean.

At this the dwarf halted his flow of enthusiasm and supressed the leap in his heart, as he did every time he heard the rustle of their bare feet on the coolness of the earth floor. He closed his eyes firmly as if this also closed his ears and steadied his heartbeat, which broke away from its usual rhythm at these unpredictable thoughts.

After a few months the dwarf found that he had become quite used to these expectant brides of Christ as they moved around him holding whispered conversations, sighing gently, smiling at him, and not concealing their bad moods in his presence. It was as if he had become one of them, and what was more he had pledged himself to the virgins, swearing that nothing would separate him from them but death. When he died he would put their love to the test. They would either return him to his family or put him in the burial chamber, where he had gone one day with the senior nun to help her sweep the floor. He wouldn't have been able to see anything, but the old woman had lit a little candle and held it up to a casket on a high wooden shelf and raised the lid. He gasped in fright at the sight of a bony frame. The ribs were plainly visible and some flesh still clung around the hands. He heard the old nun's voice whispering, "You shouldn't be frightened. You were sent to us by the Lord."

And so it was. The dwarf only looked at the iron gates occasionally, when he heard his mother's cough and knew that she still had not lost hope. At first this caused him pain, especially when he pictured her sitting on the stone where he had sat. He heard his brother calling him day after day, banging on the gates, urging him to come home. But the dwarf followed instructions, did not reply and turned back to his work. He was growing used to this obligatory link being severed, so that he could concentrate on what he wanted and not let the vibrations from the trivia of the outside world intrude and confuse him. However, when he pictured his mother and his brother taking turns to sit on the stone, he couldn't help thinking of the hoopoe and wondering whether it came to them as it used to come to him, from the direction of the green trees and the canal, or from the barren land, looking for bread crumbs.

The Land of the Sun

The car rolled over and over before it sank to the ground like a slain bird. From a distance it could have been a mirage, a vivid spot of green created by the desert in expanses of land so vast that the eye was scarcely able to take them in.

There was another, larger splash of color on the sand, from which a young man emerged, hurrying in the direction of this green spot at high speed. These were major events in this silent land, where there was nothing but the sun burning the sand tirelessly day after day, the intense shimmering brightness of mirages, the sudden gusts of wind and the night frosts.

The splash of color was made by a few tents pitched in the bare landscape of the desert, whose inhabitants, a team of hired workers roaming the sands in pursuit of creatures with unusual markings, lived a peaceful, humdrum existence, disturbed only by occasional bad dreams. These were usually the result of disappointments in their work, when the snakes and lizards escaped from the traps so painstakingly laid for them.

Jasim was the first to reach the green dot, which was still shuddering and clanking painfully. A camel lay some distance away, beating the sand in a terrifying flurry of movement like a cyclone. Its screams drowned out the sound of the liquid from the car pouring over the sand, and the faint groans of varying rhythm and pitch emerging from it.

Jasim might have stood there indefinitely, gazing in shock at the machine as if it were a species of lizard he had not seen before, but he suddenly noticed the groaning, and began trying to drag one of the passengers out through a window, his resolution hampered by the gentleness he exercised out of respect for the shattered glass, to no purpose because the window was too small to allow easy passage of the man's huge bulk. In the meantime one of his workmates arrived at a run and together they righted the car, restoring it more or less to its original position. When they had got the crumpled door open, they were brought up short by the sight of the woman in the rear passenger seat. She was moaning faintly and her clothes were rumpled and hitched up over her twisted body, exposing a large part of her stomach, while a thick plait of her hair fell around her face and over her arm, and her gold earrings were visible. Jasim glanced at his companion for a moment; then, with silent complicity, they disregarded what they had seen and devoted their energies to dragging out the driver, who appeared to be dead. They caught each other snatching a look at the woman, focusing on her bare stomach. They managed to free the child who must have been sitting next to her and had been flung against the door by the force of the collision so that fragments of his skull and brain were sticking to the side window.

Working steadily, they finally had the remaining passenger out on the burning sand in the full glare of the sun, which made the blood run more furiously and hastened their deaths. All around was calm, now that the camel had subsided and lay motionless, and the woman's moaning could still be heard from inside the car, clearer than ever.

The two youths stood quite still looking at each other,

exchanging unspoken words, and only moved to avoid the liquid that began to flow more forcefully from underneath the car. They found themselves edging farther and farther away as the flow gathered momentum, until without warning Jasim suddenly rushed back toward the car. He leaned the upper half of his body into the car with determination, and reached out his arms to take hold of the woman, but once again he was transfixed by the sight of her naked belly and her brown flesh, and the light scattering of fine hairs around her navel. He had not seen a woman's nakedness before; he hadn't seen a woman at all without yards of material wrapped around her, covering her from her head to her black-hennaed feet, and revealing only her eyes behind a gauze opening in the cloth, like two insects caught in a fishing net. So he backed away from the car. Then, as if he felt a sudden pang in his heart, he struck one palm against the other, regretting his retreat and looking at his companion in confusion, tinged with disappointment and frustration. Silently, he begged him for support, so that he would have the courage to go back and free the woman from the car.

They stood briefly together without speaking or moving, but then the strong-smelling fluid took the decision out of their hands, igniting spontaneously and in a flash transforming the car into a mirage burning in its own dryness: it was a long time since it had been filled up with water. The heat of the explosion drove the two youths away, but after a few moments they set about the task of dragging the three victims out of reach of the blazing wreck with great application, trying not to look or listen as the fire consumed the woman, although the feel of her stomach would stay with Jasim for a long time.

About the Author

One of the contemporary Arab world's most acclaimed writers, Hanan al-Shaykh grew up in Beirut. Her novels include *The Story of Zahra, Women of Sand and Myrrh, Beirut Blues* and *Only in London*. She lives in London with her husband and two children.

About the Translator

Catherine Cobham teaches Arabic at St. Andrews University, Scotland, and has translated a number of contemporary Arab writers, including Yusuf Idris, Liana Badr, and Naguib Mahfouz.

MIRA

05-
3811214

040-
5589793

23 -27.

23-25
vapaahs

ไทย

ไทย